Surge

The Storm Dragons' Mate
Book 3

M. Sinclair

Lost & Bound Publishing

Surge: *The Storm Dragons' Mate* 3

Copyright © 2023 by M. Sinclair in USA

All rights reserved.

Editorial Team:

Refined Voice Editing & Proofreading

 Formatted with Vellum

The Union of Love & Madness

Description

The man who killed my family—Linan Clanguard.

The truth radiated vibrantly in my very soul, but that gut feeling didn't provide the proof that we needed. The proof that would show he had arranged for the attack and subsequent slaughter of the entire Flash Clan.

With my mates by my side, we set off towards the rogue lands in search of the truth and end up discovering far more than we could have ever expected.

And when we uncover the real reason my clan was attacked? My worst fears come to life as I realize I'm to blame.

Surge is book 3 in the **Storm Dragons' Mate series** that features a slightly naive but sassy MFC, possessive dragon alphas, and a secret that will change everything. This is not a high school academy book, and the contents are intended for mature audiences, with characters who are all 18+. This book includes violence and mature sexual content.

Author Note:

Surge is set in the shared universe of Dark Imaginarium Academy. All series can be read independently, but characters have crossovers and it is highly encouraged to read all within the universe to understand the world in its entirety.

Series within the Universe:

Phases of the Moon by M. Sinclair
The Creatures We Crave by R.L. Caulder
The Storm Dragons' Mate by M. Sinclair
Blood Oath by R.L. Caulder

Chapter 1

Bexley Blackforge

inan Clanguard—the man who had orchestrated the death of my family.

I stood frozen in the doorway, my grip on Jagger so tight my body was shaking with tension as my watery gaze moved from my concerned mate to Linan. The malice radiating off of him had my gut twisting, and the look in his eyes was absolutely lethal, filled with hatred and the desire for pain—*my pain.*

That alone would have been enough to tell me something was wrong, but my gut was telling me it was more than that—far more than just simple 'dislike' for me.

I didn't need proof that this was the man who killed my family, but my subconscious gave it anyway. Linan Clanguard's name echoed loudly in my head, Rebecca's voice prominent above any other thought. It was from the day that I thought I lost everything, my memory and my family. With a violent tug, my magic pulled me under, lifting the heavy fog that had concealed a memory long forgotten.

I moved silently down the hall, somehow knowing that being as quiet as possible was important. I wasn't supposed to be here, but when my mom disappeared from the party, I felt the urge to leave as well—she needed me. I didn't understand why, but it felt like she did.

Moments later, after silently making my way through a dark corridor, I froze before turning the corner, the sound of harsh adult voices stopping me short.

"Leave, Linan." That was my mom's voice, but not the one I knew...it sounded so scary. I didn't think I'd ever heard her voice sound like that, and while I wasn't scared of her, a trickle of unease slithered down my spine.

A dark chuckle filled the space. "Not without my wife."

My brows knitted together, and a soft wounded sound had my chest fluttering nervously.

My mom spoke again. "Carol is staying. You weren't invited here, you are not welcome here, and you will not be taking her when you leave."

"Carol..." The man's voice was softer this time, seemingly ignoring my mom.

"Don't listen to him," my mom said soothingly but firmly.

"I won't." I didn't recognize the woman's voice. It was barely audible, a weak whisper.

"You fucking bitch," Linan snarled. "This has nothing to do with you—"

"It has everything to do with us, Clanguard," my dad snarled as he passed me in the hall, a furious energy surrounding him. His hand grazed my shoulder, a silent signal that he wanted me to stay hidden.

He had done something similar before during a conversation in his office, one where some men had been mad about something going on in the city. I'd been stuck hanging out behind his desk, quietly reading a book for what felt like hours while they argued. Despite how frustrating it was, I trusted my dad's opinion on a situation like this.

"Blackforge," Linan spit out. "I'm here to collect my wife, nothing else."

"She came to our lands, to my mate, for protection from you." My father's voice was hard. "She won't be leaving unless she wants to."

For a singular moment, I wondered if this would end with violence. I could feel it building, the turbulent magic brewing between the adults present...but all the sudden it diffused.

A large shadow stormed past me without a word. I reared back, slapping a hand over my mouth as I sank against the wall, glad Clanguard hadn't seen me as he disappeared down the dark corridor. I could tell he was scared, and even though he hadn't exactly run down the hallway, his steps were far too brisk to be casual.

The second he was far enough away for it to feel safe, I turned the corner and stepped into the room, anxious to be safe from that Clanguard man's eyes if he decided to look back.

"Carol." My mom's voice was filled with emotion. "You're safe here. I don't care what we have to do, we won't let him take you."

"Mom? Dad?" I called out. My dad offered me a sad smile that didn't match the anger in his gaze. My own moved to the unfamiliar woman my mom was comforting.

I inhaled sharply. Her small frame was wrapped in a cotton dress and shawl, slippers on her feet, and her pretty auburn hair contrasted the purple and blue marks that marred every inch of visible skin.

Her dark eyes met mine, their depths containing

such an intense sadness that it rocked me. I opened my mouth to say something, but a sob bubbled up from her throat as she buried her face against my mom's shoulder, making me feel immensely guilty. I took a step back, feeling a bit weak in the knees at the idea of making her cry—

"Bex, this is Carol. She's going to be staying with us for a bit," my mom explained, her eyes filled with understanding. "You didn't make her cry. I promise. She just misses—"

"My son." Carol inhaled and tried to stop crying, although I didn't know why. Crying was a good thing if you were sad, especially if it made you feel better. I watched her wipe her tears away. "My son, Fletcher. He's close to your age."

"He's not with you?"

Carol shook her head and offered a small smile. "He's safe at home."

He was safe there, but she wasn't? I didn't understand.

"I'm going to close out this little event," my dad stated, extending a hand to me. "Why don't you come with me, kiddo, and leave Mom to walk Carol back to her room."

"Okay." I nodded, feeling uneasy with this situation. "It was nice to meet you."

Those didn't feel like the right words at all, but I didn't have better ones.

"Same." Carol put a watery smile on her face, and as we walked away, my dad's expression darkened. When we turned the corner and made our way down the hall, he finally stopped and crouched down, holding my hand.

"What's wrong?" I frowned, not liking the expression on his face.

"Promise me, Bex, that if you ever see that man again, you will run."

"Run?" I felt my brows go up. "You said we don't run—we're dragons. We fly."

My dad almost smiled, but his eyes were too sad for that. "Fly or run, just get away from him. Promise me."

"I promise you, Dad."

And now I was breaking my promise.

Unintentionally, of course. But as I stood here, Jagger's hands on either side of my cheeks as he spoke to me in soft tones, the words not translating in my head, I found I couldn't move. I couldn't focus on anything but Linan Clanguard. The man had caused so much pain, so much devastation in my life.

Rebecca's voice now twined with my father's, playing loudly in my head like a broken record.

"I need you to remember one thing, though. No matter what happens, there is one person you have to avoid—Linan Clanguard."

"Promise me, Bex, that if you ever see that man again, you will run."

Again and again. So much so that my head began to pulse in pain. They had both warned me of Linan, and now I knew why he'd had a motive to hurt my parents—Carol.

"What's going on?" Gage asked, the panic in his voice finally succeeding in breaking through the haze of shock.

I blinked, moving my gaze to the heir of the Bronzeheart estate as a warm rough hand slid up my back—Breaker. My mates. All three of them were staring at me in surprise, and I found myself voiceless, unable to tell them what was wrong for so many reasons, and not just having to do with Linan being feet away.

That thought had my brain clicking back on, and I tried to school my reaction. I couldn't let him know that I knew—a gut instinct warned me of his possible reaction. Hopefully I was doing a better job at hiding my emotions than normal—as my mates had pointed out before, my face revealed *everything*. Maybe I could say something to shift any suspicion he may have that I remembered him or suspected his involvement in their loss. My mind was moving a million miles an hour, and none of my thoughts were helping the panic trying to claw at my throat.

"Is everything okay?" Professor Clanguard's voice was cautious and concerned, everyone in the room staring at me in confusion.

Literally, the room of twenty something men and women gathered alongside a few professors along the back wall were staring at me, waiting for an answer. All of them had gathered here to talk about us being...mates? That was weird, right? I felt like this was a weird conversation to have, even if they were masking it under the concept of an equality of power or something along those lines.

"Yes," I answered before my mates could. "I just felt a bit overwhelmed by how many people are here —it's been a lot the past few days."

It wasn't a lie, and the knot in my chest began to relax as at least half the room began to nod in understanding. I avoided looking at Linan though. I didn't like the idea of them viewing me as weak or easily overwhelmed, especially as I learned what a big deal that was in shifter culture, but at least here it would play to my advantage.

"Right." Professor Clanguard motioned to the

front of the room where a long table with four chairs sat facing everyone else. "Please take a seat. Hopefully this won't take long."

The end of his statement was tinged with hope, but I worried it was misguided. These people had traveled all the way to DIA for a meeting—call me crazy, but I had a feeling they wouldn't be leaving until they felt like they had fully gotten their reassurance.

Taking a shaky breath, I felt relieved as Gage slid a hand along my lower back and led me towards one of the center chairs, taking the outside seat while my other two mates sat to the left of me. I was comfortably insulated between the three of them, and their familiar scents had my dragon—who I was now fully able to recognize as an entity in its own right—calming despite the possible threat in the room.

There were murmurs throughout the room, no doubt about our dynamic, but I couldn't help but look up at Gage instead of listening to them, finding him already staring down at me. His emerald eyes were dark, swirling with bronze streaks that made my chest warm. I used to associate them with his dragon, and while it totally had to do with his magic, it also had a lot to do with his reaction to me. My toes curled thinking about just how reactive Gage was towards me during our moment in the caves...

My cheeks flushed as a low rumble left his throat, his hand tightening on my upper thigh. The man was stacked with muscles at 6'6", and the grip he had on me sometimes was enough to turn me into absolute putty. Then again, everything about the man did distracting things to me.

Right now, his dark hair was messy—the reddish undertones highlighted in the awful lighting of the conference room—and his skin almost looked like it had a slight hint of gold or bronze. His jawline, normally clean shaven, had a hint of stubble, and I could see the past few days—well, honestly all the days since we'd arrived here—had weighed on him. He was exhausted, and while things had changed in the best of ways, things were also coming to light that weren't nearly as easy to handle.

"We can leave," he said softly, as if reading my mind. "Say the word and we're out of here."

"Gage," Jagger warned, making me realize the room had quieted and his words had been heard. I didn't think Jagger disagreed, but it wouldn't help for anyone else to know that. My mates' intense loyalty to me was the exact thing this crowd was worried about, wasn't it?

Or maybe Jagger wasn't worried about that at all.

I mean, he might be saying *'You're right, let's get out of here,'* because the way he was staring at the crowd was anything but nice. I wasn't positive what it would feel like to be at the receiving end of that look, but I had to assume it wouldn't be good—not good at all.

His silver hair streaked with black was slicked back, and his dark clothing made his skin look icy, like his blue eyes. I decided to take a risk, wanting to soothe the tension in his jawline, and ran my finger along the rune right there. His gaze shot down to me and he offered a small smile, attempting to look unbothered, but I knew that was far from the case.

All my mates hated the idea of us being here.

I didn't love it either, but if it meant avoiding future problems, especially for their families outside of DIA... Well, I was telling myself I could deal with it. I wasn't sure how true that was, though, given the sick, twisted feeling in my stomach and the fact that seeing Clanguard was making me furiously angrily, to the point that I was nearly shaking.

I wasn't very good at hiding either extreme emotion, so focusing on my mates kept my eyes off of Clanguard, which was a very good idea right now.

"Is this going to be a problem?" Professor Clanguard asked. I stared at him with wide eyes, realizing that Rachel's mate looked just like Carol—his mother. Where Fletcher looked a lot like Linan, the professor looked like their mother. Although their hair color was opposite...

I blinked and shook my head, trying to refocus.

"Depends if they decide to behave themselves," Breaker rumbled, looking completely unbothered by the speculative looks everyone else was offering us. Or maybe they were cautious because of the mood my mates were in.

Breaker's gaze moved to mine, his unique eyes—one completely black and the other gold—sparkling with an intensity that reminded me of sparks on metal. His blonde hair was messy, and the scar on his face, plus the ones that I knew ran down his body, made him look like a warrior. There was something wild about Breaker but at the same time so completely sweet, like he was my own teddy bear.

Although his dragon would probably hate that.

Or maybe he would love it. I mean, they had gotten me stuffed dragons recently...

"Right..." Professor Clanguard cleared his throat and pulled everyone's attention to the front of the room. "If we're ready to begin—I'm Professor Thomas Clanguard, the shifter sector leader at DIA."

Even though he wasn't alpha to this pack, the way everyone immediately focused on him made it clear they respected him.

"All of you traveled—without warning—because of your concern and mistrust—"

"I wouldn't call it mistrust!" A man raised his voice, his eyes darting across my mates. "Call it concern."

"Bullshit," Gage said evenly, making my brows rise in surprise.

"As I said," Professor Clanguard continued, "concern *and* mistrust. Label it however you want, you all have come here to question the four of them, and they have *chosen* to entertain your inquiry. They are not only welcome to leave at any time, but as students are protected and have the right to feel safe in their own temporary home."

"Come now, son." Linan Clanguard stood, looking suddenly far more friendly. "No need to talk about safety. We aren't threatening them, we are here simply to ensure some things."

"To ensure what?" Jagger asked knowingly.

Linan's hands spread out dramatically. "We are here to ensure that the balance of power within Trabea is maintained."

Something told me that Clanguard didn't want balance, though. He wanted the scales tipped —*towards him.*

Chapter 2

Bexley Blackforge

"Hold on, Linan."

A female voice drew everyone's attention away from the man in question, his nose scrunching at the use of his first name. He probably wanted to be addressed as 'Alpha Clanguard.' Whatever the case, I felt like I could breathe again now that his attention was diverted, and I hoped that maybe—just maybe—not everyone would have the same volatile aggression as the wolf alpha.

I was coming to understand that was normal in the shifter world, but I didn't have to like it, and I sure as heck wasn't comfortable with it.

Linan, maybe being polite or maybe in a more sarcastic manner, waved his hand, as if giving the woman permission to speak. Although I didn't think that she cared what he wanted because she wasn't even looking at him—she was looking right at *me*.

"Before we explore the full dynamic of what's going on, I think it's only fair that the four of them—especially Bexley Blackforge—know who's talking to her."

That would be nice.

Especially since the woman's gaze was soft towards me. Friendly. There was something regal about her, her lithe frame and angled features posed almost perfectly with her hair brushed over her shoulder in an elegant wave. I had no idea what type of shifter she was, though—there were no striking features that reminded me of any particular animal.

Then again, it wasn't like my mates and I looked like dragons...well, for the most part. I suppose the gold sparkle embedded in my skin wasn't exactly 'normal.'

Also, *Bexley Blackforge* was so odd to hear, even after everything I'd learned.

"Agreed," the man next to her said.

The woman gave him an affectionate smile before continuing. "I'm Chanelle Spencer, Alpha for the avian shifters in the city. It's a pleasure to meet you."

Avian. So they were birds? What type of birds?

Dragons and birds were similar in some senses. I mean, we did both fly...

"Bexley," I offered lamely, although it was very clear she knew who I was.

"And this is my mate, Kelvin." She placed a delicate hand on his shoulder, the man as delicately built as her but far taller. To the point that he was almost eye to eye with her, even though he was sitting down. I offered a small nod in greeting.

"Unlike some of us here"—her gaze flickered over to Linan—"we don't believe there is a conspiracy afoot, and I don't want you thinking that the entire city is against you. Often in moments like this, silent support means nothing when you have such outspoken dissent."

Oh. That was unexpected. A small smile slipped onto my lips.

Her gaze moved to the boys. "Gentlemen, I believe I've met each of you and your parents. Please don't let our presence here be a signifier of our unhappiness with the current standing. I want you to know you have support."

"And they clearly know it now," Linan drew out, making the woman's eyes narrow.

"Thank you, Alpha Spencer. We appreciate it," Jagger said, Breaker and Gage both offering nods of agreement as she sat and looked towards the other leaders in the room expectantly.

"Right." A young man with completely black eyes and icy skin stood, looking uncomfortable. His hair was slicked back, and he looked at my mates, seemingly trying to convey something silently for a long moment, before looking at me.

"Ciaran Bowman, Alpha to the water shifters. I came here suspecting the worst, but after talking to my brother, I realized I may have been mistaken. Not because of the possible power issue—that still concerns me—but because I've been made aware that Bexley here has stood up for shifters, specifically prey shifters."

I was beyond curious who his brother was... maybe Erty, the shark shifter I'd met at the party and then during the confrontation in the courtyard? The one who had a problem with Fletcher's beta? They looked very similar so it wouldn't surprise me if they were related.

"To gain their allegiance?" someone asked, sounding half curious. It was the same man that had shouted out before.

"I'm not sure," Ciaran admitted, looking towards me for answers.

Gage's hand squeezed my leg in support as I

tried to muster my confidence to reply. "No, it wasn't for allegiance. I don't even know most of their names."

"So why then?" Ciaran frowned.

"Well..." I nibbled my lip. "Honestly? Because I'm not okay with bullying someone just because they're perceived as weaker than you. It's unnecessary and cruel. Everyone is aware of the 'hierarchy' that exists, there's no need to take advantage and physically hurt those who are supposedly weaker shifters than you."

Shocked silence, something I should have expected but hadn't, filled the space. Even Chanelle's brows were up in surprise as Jagger squeezed my hand in support, my chest tightening with nervousness.

"Are you for fucking real?" a deep voice demanded, drawing my attention towards the back of the room where a large man—I mean *really* large— stood surrounded by men and women of similar size.

"William, do *not* talk to my mate like that." Breaker's chair nearly fell over as he jumped to his feet, his voice brooking no argument. The harshness and dominance caused a shiver of pleasure to roll over my skin.

I also could tell, and I wasn't positive how, that this William individual was a bear shifter. I think it was his magic, or maybe his energy? But I could practically see the bear residing inside of him, running under his skin. Why hadn't I been able to do that with Alpha Spencer?

The man put his hands up and grunted, clearly realizing he'd misstepped and feeling the power from my mates saturate the room as he leaned forward over the table. "Breaker, this shit sounds ridiculous. You're telling me that a female storm dragon, mated to the three of you, doesn't believe in power structures?"

"It's easy to say when you are at the top." The soft words came from the woman sitting next to the man who'd questioned why I was helping prey shifters.

Deciding I needed to step in, I stood up and spoke directly to William. "I understand that's not how things work in the shifter world, but I don't have that same mindset. Until recently, I wasn't even aware I was a dragon." I paused for a moment, exhaling before I continued. "The point is, I don't buy into it. I don't like it. You can believe me or you can choose not to, but if I see something I don't like, I will always step in."

"And how many times have you stepped in?" William asked, frowning.

"I'm not sure, a few—"

"Apparently quite a few times," Ciaran explained. I sat down slowly, my bravery fading along with my indignation.

"I think we've fallen off topic," Linan tried to suggest but instead the woman from before stood up, tilting her head as her short dark hair seemed to shimmer around her delicate features. There was something familiar about her but I couldn't figure out what...

"Annika. I'm one of the council leaders for the prey community in the city," she said, ignoring Linan. Which was clearly uncomfortable for her, because her body language was shying away from him. Also, I noticed that she hadn't said 'alpha,' she'd said 'council leader.' Was that how they did things in their community?

"Most of our kind live outside of the city in clan land," she continued to explain. "I'll be the first to admit that the dragon clans protect prey shifters as a whole, but I find it hard to believe that you think so differently from them. Your mates are known for being ruthless—"

"Please stop," I said calmly, feeling a weird defensive urge roll over me. "I don't need to hear that. I know who my mates are, who they truly are, and I know—or am at least figuring out—who I am. If you're questioning them, then question them, but

I'm my own person. All I can tell you is that I don't like how things are currently."

"And *that* is my exact problem," Linan announced, Annika's annoyance with him clear as she offered me a cautious nod and sat down. Clanguard stood and spread his hands on the table as if he was trying to take up as much space as possible.

"She just said it! She doesn't like the norm, the status quo, and that means change—change that comes in the form of an alliance between four storm dragons and three powerful clans. For the longest time, the city has existed as a separate part of Trabea, but who's to say that will remain the case?"

"What are you saying?" Gage demanded, his voice full of power.

"I'm saying that I believe you four will come to the city center and try to take it." His words were final and hard, and when I looked towards the others, I saw...well, it wasn't agreement. Not exactly. Maybe from William, but the others looked more cautious and confused than anything, waiting for my answer.

"Why would we do that?" Jagger asked curiously.

"We have more than enough land and more than enough responsibility," Breaker added.

"Yes," Clanguard snapped. "In fact, between the

three of you, you rule at least eighty percent of the territory."

"What exactly do you want, Linan?" Gage drew out, his words dark. "We aren't going to sit here and beg you to trust us. Hell, I'm not asking for your trust to begin with. I am telling you, we are perfectly content with the land already entrusted to us. We don't want anything to do with the city."

"And what about her?" he demanded. "Black-forge, what about you?"

"I don't want any land in the city." I frowned, trying to ignore my fury as I focused on the rest of the room. "I'm not sure why you're being like this in the first place." Deciding to extend a hand, I looked to the other leaders present. "What would make all of you feel more secure in this situation?'"

Linan looked around the room before narrowing his gaze on me, answering my question even though it hadn't been directed to him. "There is something you could do to eliminate our concerns, a compromise that would allow us to have more space, and it would be a show of good faith."

I could feel my men tensing. I hesitated, knowing I wasn't going to like what he had to say. "And what's that?"

"We take the rogue lands."

The Flash Clan lands—the Blackforge lands.

I didn't know how to describe the urge rolling through me, but it was uncontrollable. "Absolutely not. Those lands are mine."

My words radiated with power, and I knew it was my dragon forcing the declaration from my chest, but I didn't disagree. It was *my* family lands, and my men agreed with me. I could feel it through our bonds, which radiated with approval at my strength.

Not everyone felt the same.

"See! Power hungry," Linan growled in victory. It was infuriating, especially considering what I knew he'd done to my family.

"Not power hungry," I gritted out. "Those are my family's—the Flash Clan's—lands."

"Land that has sat unclaimed for some time," Ciaran pointed out, looking conflicted.

"While you were stashed away somewhere—"

"Shut it," Gage warned William who nearly rolled his eyes.

My gaze darted around the room as I decided to reveal a little bit of what I'd gone through and how we'd gotten to this point. Maybe then, the others would understand.

"I was kept safe by the Bronzehearts," I said to William. "Until recently, I had no memory of my past life. It wasn't until I shifted that I even realized I was a dragon. The Bronzehearts kept me safe from those who attacked my family—those who *killed* my family. So yes, those lands have sat unclaimed because until this past week, I didn't know I had a family, let alone land."

"Bexley doesn't owe any of you this," Jagger said with forced calm, his voice dripping with disgust. "In fact, we don't owe you this meeting to begin with—so do not take her words lightly."

"Those lands rightfully belong to her," Breaker added in solidarity.

"You only found out about your power and the loss of your parents this week?" Chanelle's voice was soft and filled with concern.

"Yes. It's been over eight years," I whispered. "I didn't even remember Jagger or Breaker—and being told anything about my past caused immense pain."

I wasn't going to spell out that I'd had a spell on my memories that locked them away from me, but I also felt like they needed to know at least some of it so they didn't blame the Bronzehearts for not telling me.

"And then we came here questioning you," Annika said, her gaze hardening as she turned to address Linan. "Clanguard, this is wrong. This was a fucked-up idea."

"I agree," Ciaran said.

"I will admit that maybe we should have waited," William muttered, but literally no one paid attention to him. I couldn't tell what I thought about him.

"Who killed them?" Chanelle asked. "I heard no one was ever found—do you remember? Better yet, how did you survive?"

"I don't know," I admitted, trying to not look at Linan. It was the perfect moment to hide what I knew, and I was going to take it until we could figure out a full plan.

Then he had to open his mouth.

"The Blackforges had many enemies," he spat. "They kidnapped my own wife at one point."

I narrowed my eyes, feeling thunder roll under my skin, threatening to break out. I could tell he was watching my reaction. "You don't know anything about my parents," I said through gritted teeth.

"I know more than you, little girl," he snarled. "They deserved to be slaughtered—"

I couldn't explain what happened next. It was like an out-of-body experience. One moment I was standing behind the table next to my mates, and the next I was across the room in front of Linan, my hand thrust forward as voltage surged through me. With every part of my being, every fiber of it, I planned on hurting him. *Really* hurting him. Cutting him deep like his words cut me—

An arm caught around my waist and pulled me back, but it didn't break me from the haze that had fallen over me. It was like the creature inside of me exploded, and electricity danced across my skin as I went to the floor with whichever of my mates had grabbed me. My ears were ringing, and heat seared my flesh. Gage was holding me tight, his voice calling for me, but all I could see was a haze of power.

I was shaking so bad, and I could taste blood in my mouth, the trembling causing me to bite the inside of my mouth. I felt like I was melting and burning in an inferno of my own making.

A noise left my throat, a vicious roar, and I knew without a doubt that absolute chaos was exploding around me.

Then everything went dark.

I couldn't tell you how long I existed like that, in absolute silence. Eventually, though, I heard a familiar voice. Eventually I heard my mate.

"Wake up, little treasure," Jagger said gently. "I need you to wake up."

I couldn't ignore the demand in his voice, and my eyes fluttered open to find him in front of me, my body propped up against Gage's chest as Breaker crouched in my peripheral. Jagger's intense gaze wasn't what caught my attention though...

No, what caught my attention was the room.

The room was absolutely destroyed, the walls stained with soot and the floors strewn with shrapnel from broken chairs and tables. Like something had exploded in here.

Something *had* exploded. *I exploded.*

The worst part? I didn't know what had happened to everyone else in the room.

Chapter 3

Gage Bronzeheart

My cupcake was *so* incredibly powerful. That word didn't do justice to how strong Bexley was, though, and what she could do if provoked—what she *had* done.

I watched transfixed as she looked around the seared room in shock that slowly transformed into horror. Her face, which had been flushed and now was covered in ash, turned icy pale.

It was my first clue that she was about to pass out.

Luckily, I caught her in my arms the minute her body slumped. I wasn't surprised that she went unconscious but it still concerned me, knowing that she must have been extremely overwhelmed for that to have happened.

Tucking her against me, I glowered at the side

door that swung open, revealing everyone who'd run to hide from her explosive power, including that fucker Linan.

Of course, I was glad they'd hidden—at least some of them—or else they would've been destroyed along with the rest of the charred room. Fucking Linan would have been no loss though. In fact, the only thing that was stopping me from going after him right now was the way Bexley had melted into me, her even breathing portraying how exhausted the display of power had rendered her.

And fuck did that not surprise me.

Her emotions had ignited a flame—literally—that had turned the room into a vision of a fiery inferno of black and red. Her skin had turned into black scales with fire running along it, making it look like the flames were eating her alive—but I knew she probably hadn't felt it. Jagger, Breaker, and I hadn't felt it either, our bond with her protecting us from the flames.

"This! This is the—"

Breaker flashed across the space and slammed Linan against the wall by the throat, knocking the man out instantly from the force of the impact of his head hitting the wall.

Silence permeated the space and I spoke in a hard tone, hoping to make myself extremely clear.

"We are leaving—*now*. We came here in a show of good faith, and instead Linan took the opportunity to not only insinuate my mate was lying about her intentions towards prey shifters, but to insult her dead parents."

"Thomas, I would highly suggest informing Fletcher of what your father did," Jagger said in a voice that was far calmer than I knew he was feeling, the only hint of his anger found in his use of Professor Clanguard's first name.

In fact, because Bexley had marked all of us, I felt more connected than ever to the two men I considered brothers—and they were fucking furious.

"Of course." Professor Clanguard smirked, clearly relishing in his father's fate.

Breaker stepped back and looked at all of them. "As for the rest of you, take this as a warning. Trust us or not, we keep our word, and anyone who questions it or threatens to take Bexley's lands from her will end up in far worse shape than Linan is in now."

Pulling Bexley further against me while straightening myself up from the ground, I turned from the room and walked out. I wanted her as far as possible from Linan, and I hoped that when he woke up he realized what a mistake he'd made. My eyes drifted down to Bexley's face, remembering what she'd said to Jagger.

"*That's the name. That's the name from the memory. I think...I think that's the man who killed my family.*"

"Not yet," Jagger said quietly, as if reading my mind.

I knew he was right, and as we left through the halls, walking quietly, the cool afternoon weather turned crisper as the distant sound of thunder had me exhaling in relief. It wasn't a moment to feel any sense of relief, but the storm would help her replenish her magic faster.

The campus was quiet, the Thursday evening atmosphere taking on a far more tense note than it had before the meeting. Bexley murmured something against my neck but didn't wake, making me worry even more. I could feel her dragon under her skin, but her magic almost felt like an extinguished flame.

Then a rumble of thunder rolled through the stormy skies above.

Like a lightning bolt had struck her, Bexley tensed in my arms before a small sigh left her plush lips. Droplets of rain began to come down as we made our way down the forested path to our dorm, and I nearly smiled as her ash-covered skin began to glow its normal luminescent shade, freckled with what appeared to be actual gold.

My cupcake was painfully beautiful, even covered in ash—maybe more so—her gold silk hair falling over my arm like a curtain and her small curvy frame tucked against me perfectly. Luckily, unlike last time, her clothes were relatively unharmed, as if her magic had protected them—although they were also covered in ash. I would have really killed those fuckers in that meeting if she'd been naked and they'd had the honor of seeing her like that.

No one but her mates deserved to see her that way. Hell, maybe not even us.

A near rumble broke from my throat thinking about the last time I'd seen her naked, of taking Bexley and marking her as my mate. It was impossible to describe the primal satisfaction that it left me with; the only word I could think of that came close was *completion*.

It was everything I had always wanted with Bexley but feared I would never have.

Which is also why I was determined to protect our peace—our new family dynamic and our future. I would do anything to keep her happy.

"Gage?" Bexley's lashes fluttered, her eyes' gold nature flashing metallic under the stormy sky. As thunder rumbled again and we finally reached our dorm complex, I kept her close against me and whispered that we were almost home. She nodded in understanding and closed her eyes once again, and I fought the urge to kiss the freckles on her nose as we stepped into the elevator that led up to her room.

As the doors closed and I sagged against the wall, the three of us offered one another expressions of commiseration. That meeting had been exactly as I'd feared—complete bullshit.

"She should explain what she saw," Jagger said as he stared down at our mate. "The vision she had. But she believes that Linan is the reason for her parents' death."

What the fuck?

"I'm going to get her washed off and comfortable," I said quietly. "This storm is going to recharge her power really fast...hopefully."

"I'll make her something to eat," Breaker said, frowning as he looked over at her. I knew exactly what he was seeing—how delicate she looked in this state.

"I'm going to grab some of the shit from my dorm, some documents regarding our family and the book that your mom gave her," Jagger murmured. "I want to see why Clanguard would do something like that, besides the obvious."

Power.

Bexley murmured something so softly I couldn't

hear it as the elevator doors opened and we walked into the main room of her dorm. I went straight into the bathroom and turned on the shower, then stripped her clothes off as she stood on unsteady feet, looking super out of it as her eyes blinked open. I knew it would be hard—fucking literally—with both of us naked in the shower, especially because my dragon was constantly reminding me of how good it felt to mate with her, but we had ash all over ourselves that we needed to get rid of. Plus, I craved to hold her, to have that skin-to-skin contact, more than anything right now. Especially with how concerned I was about her.

As the water steamed up the room, I gently led her under the spray and got to work washing her hair and body. She hummed under her breath as I worked, not fully present. It was after about ten minutes of washing her and then myself that she seemed to fully register what was happening, wrapping her arms around my waist and burying her head in my chest.

When a pained noise left her throat, I pulled back to see tears welling in her eyes.

"Gage," she whispered, looking panicked and pale once again. Fuck, I hoped she didn't pass out in the shower. My concern was enough I nearly turned off the water and lifted her out of there.

"Breathe." I infused my voice with a command I wouldn't normally use, but it had the desired effect. Her eyes fluttered open, trying to focus on me. "Everything is okay. You're okay, we're okay, and unfortunately—at least in the case of Linan—everyone survived."

"Oh, thank the fates." Bexley's voice broke as tears trailed down her cheeks. "I thought...when I saw the empty room...I thought the worst."

"Everyone is fine," I reassured her, brushing my lips against hers. "I promise you, everything is going to be okay, Bexley."

A shuddering breath left her as she nodded, offering no other response. She closed her eyes and let the water stream over her, caught up in her thoughts, and I had a feeling which memory she'd been pulled into. I hadn't realized in the moment what was happening, but seeing Linan had clearly been enough to trigger the answer to the question we'd had for some time now.

Who had killed the Blackforge family?

* * *

"Linan Clanguard. He's the one responsible, I'm almost positive—no, not *almost*. I am positive." Bexley paced in front of the fireplace, her body rigid with tension. The movement was so unlike my cupcake, I had to force myself to not reach forward and pull her onto my lap just to feel her soft skin again. After showering and eating, the four of us were sitting around Bex's living room, and she had just explained her memory in full.

The memory that explained everything yet proved...well, nothing. It did in a sense, in that it provided all the motive in the world—I mean, the bastard had even mentioned his wife being 'kid-napped' by the Blackforge family in the meeting. The man was a walking red flag in my book.

"It sounds like he has the damn motive," Breaker said, running a hand over his face. "I wonder what caused her to go to your family—what was the connection? Why them?"

"His wife was from the same town as Bexley's mom," Jagger said, looking up from the book my mom had made for Bex. "She isn't mentioned much, but Gage's mom wrote down a list of people from their hometown they kept in contact with. Her last name was Clanguard when this was written, but I can't tell when that was, and there aren't any other notes about her."

I would ask my mom about that the next time I talked to her.

"He admitted it so easily, it makes me wonder

why he would do that, especially while talking about your parents' death." I frowned, feeling like there was something I was missing.

Bexley's brows dipped. "I thought that was odd too. I mean, unless he was trying to make me angry? Provoke a reaction? He seemed angry himself, but he doesn't seem like the type to—"

"Lose his cool after orchestrating the meeting himself?" Breaker asked. "I would agree with that. I think this was all planned, even him mentioning that. I'm not sure what he's after, but I don't think it's as simple as your family's lands."

"It's true he's had years to try to claim them." I ran a hand through my hair, trying to sort through my thoughts on the situation. "There has to be something more to this."

"I think there is," Jagger agreed. "There has to be a bigger picture. If Bexley's memory serves correctly, his wife ran because of physical abuse or something along those lines. Which aligns with the rumors we had heard about their pack."

"The rumors on how the women in their pack were treated were..." Bad? That didn't seem like a good enough way to describe the rumored abuse and human rights violations that had taken place.

Not finishing my muttered sentence, I held Bexley's gaze, hoping she didn't ask me to explain.

The things I'd heard the Clanguards engaged in with their women, from buying and selling, to even worse, were not things I liked to keep in my mind.

"Maybe...maybe my mom found out about it through Carol?"

Bexley's words had my thoughts churning. "Like she confirmed it and your family tried to take action?"

"There's nothing written down about that, but it wouldn't be out of character for the clans to step in if that had been brought to their attention," Breaker agreed.

"And that would have caused the Clanguard pack to attack your parents because they were threatening to upend their society," Jagger finished.

It made sense. It was extreme, but that was also exactly how someone like Clanguard would conduct business—hell, that was how most wolves were.

"I wish I could remember more about the night I lost my memories," Bex mumbled, wringing her hands together. "I wish I could trigger more memories about my parents and that time in general. It would be so helpful, and we wouldn't be stuck guessing on everything."

An idea occurred to me as I looked at the storming sky outside, noticing the way the lightning and thunder seemed to be growing more intense, possibly because of our emotions. I knew it was possible for storm dragons to influence the weather, but usually it took a lot of power.

I suppose four heirs would do the trick.

"Let's go to your old home—the rogue lands." Maybe it would jog some memories. Either way, it couldn't really hurt.

All three of them looked at me in surprise before Bexley was nodding, a small, eager smile pulling at her lips. "I love that idea for a lot of reasons—and I think it'll work."

"It's a good idea," Jagger agreed. "While we're out, we may also want to talk to the other city leaders separately, without the influence of Linan nearby."

"Our parents can handle that..." Breaker said, thinking out loud. "But it may be best if we do it directly, unless they see a reason why that would be bad."

"We should definitely get their advice," Bexley said as she looked out the window. "When...when can we go?"

"We need to get to the portal. Let me arrange some stuff, and we'll finalize everything with the headmistress in the morning." I pulled her hand gently so that she stood in front of me, the other two occupying themselves by talking about the city leaders. Some of whom I really had a huge fucking issue with—like William.

"Until then," I continued, "you need to get some sleep."

"Not going to happen." She smiled slightly, but there was tension in her gaze as she looked up again to the windows that made up her ceiling and curved down to the back wall of her dorm. "It's storming; I'm full of energy."

"We could stay up and watch movies," Jagger suggested. "That way you don't have to sleep but you're still resting."

Great fucking idea, because I knew for a fact that while her power may have been fueling her, she was going to crash, and crash hard. The magic she'd used was more than even *I* would feel comfortable using without resting afterwards.

I knew the control of her magic was something we needed to work on, purely for her own safety, but I also loved her raw use of it because it came so naturally to her.

"Fine." Bexley sighed with mock annoyance. "But I get to pick which movie."

I couldn't help but smile. I had watched all of Bexley's favorite movies, but the others hadn't except for once—and I had a feeling they didn't realize what they were in for.

Chapter 4

Bexley Blackforge

The room was chilled, almost to the point that I was shivering while curled up between my parents. My dragon was silent in my chest, afraid to move or even make a noise, not wanting to draw any attention to me. Especially from the woman at the front of the room—the entire reason we were here—who was creating a spectacular display of lights and magic over an altar covered in candles and herbs.

Something I would normally love...but I could feel the tension between my parents, and the way they were keeping me so close worried me. Something significant was going on, and while I didn't understand it fully, I did know that we'd been called here by this woman because of me. But so far all she said was that she had information about my future.

Normally I would have loved this type of thing. We had several prophetesses in our clan, and most of the time I enjoyed watching their spells and shows they put on. Especially when what they had to say was good—like an upcoming season of storms, because that meant a lot of flying.

But tonight didn't have the same feeling.

"What is she doing?" my dad asked under his breath. My mom's brow contorted in confusion, then she shrugged. That didn't make me feel better at all.

"I don't know," my mom admitted quietly. "I really don't know why we're even here—"

"Four lines!" The woman's voice echoed through the room as she froze, her hands raised in front of her in a spooky effect as smoke filled the room, bringing with it the faint scent of a bonfire. Then it suddenly disappeared, and my eyes widened as the woman's gaze turned cloudy.

She continued. "Four lines united by one."

My mom's hand rubbed my back gently and the tension in the air eased, as if what she was saying made my parents happy. Or maybe not happy...but it wasn't as bad as they thought it would be. I looked between them before looking back at the woman.

Silence filled the space before her hand came down and pointed right at me.

"One that will threaten everything."

That didn't sound good.

Before my parents could say or do anything, a violent scream filled the room. I cried out and curled in on myself as the walls shook and my ears rang. Shock permeated through every nerve ending as I felt my dad wrap his arms around me.

The wailing continued, louder and more powerful, as my mom shouted something.

A piece of rubble fell right in front of us, the walls themselves falling in response to the magic surging through the room. Magic that claimed one would threaten everything—

A cry caught in my throat as I flung straight up in bed. My entire body was shaking with tension, sweat prickling the back of my neck, and my skin was lit with a fiery sensation like flames were rolling beneath it. My head was pounding, and my stomach churned. I flung myself to the edge of the bed and heaved, nearly throwing up right on the ground.

Holy crap.

Letting out a groan, I sank against the mattress, feeling like the world was spinning around me. My body was trembling as I reached out and grabbed one of my six stuffed dragons, burying my nose against its plush body as I curled up on my side. I wasn't positive where my mates were, but the plushies went a long way to making me feel better.

Especially because it was so clear that the memory I'd just experienced had been...tainted? That was the only word I had for it. Something was off.

Four lines united by one...who threatens everything.

That was all I had to work with, and I had absolutely no idea what the heck that meant.

Considering the woman had been pointing right at me, I guess I could be considered the 'one' and the four lines were the Storm Dragon Clans? That sounded right. But 'threaten everything'? What the heck was I threatening?

Eventually rolling onto my back, I couldn't help but appreciate the rain rolling down the wall of windows that made up the back wall of my bedroom and arched to the ceiling in a greenhouse effect. It was beautiful. Heck, this entire dorm was perfection, and the massive circular bed I was on, covered in sheets of pink and gold, was all the reason I needed in the world to get up—to ensure I didn't freakin' throw up on it. I just needed the strength to actually sit up...

"Little treasure?" Jagger's familiar voice filled my

dorm, loud enough I could hear it from the main room.

"Jagger?" I called out, looking towards the door as I struggled to sit up. His hypnotic gaze instantly ran over me and heat flashed there...before turning to concern.

"What's wrong?" I blinked as he appeared right at my bedside and gently cupped my jaw. It was such a soft, sweet action that I couldn't help but melt into it, loving the way the intense man touched me. I swear, he had all the control in the world and absolutely none. Well, when it came to me.

I loved it.

"I had a weird dream," I murmured. "I should wait till I can tell everyone, but it was with my parents and a prophetess that we had back home..."

Jagger's brows shot up. "I'd heard the Blackforge clan used prophetesses for a lot of their decisions, but I never had confirmation."

"This wasn't even a decision, either. This was a weird prophecy," I mumbled, wondering if I needed to write it down to remember it in full.

"Do you want to try and get some more sleep first?" Jagger asked softly. "We can tell the others when they get back. It's pretty damn early, so I figured you would be sleeping for a while more. They went to get some breakfast to bring back here."

"No sleep." I sat forward so I was on the edge of the bed and his large body was between my bare legs, my body covered with only a shirt. Something that should have made me blush, but I still felt so dazed that I could only focus on the way he kept his large arms on either side of my hips and continued to watch me with worry. "I need to get up and move around. I feel less rested than when I first went to bed."

"I bet." He frowned, running a hand over the ends of my hair, which hung to my waist. "You were tossing and turning all night."

"Is that why they went to get breakfast?" I asked. "We could have gone; I could have woken up sooner."

"We could have," Jagger said, "but it's been storming most of the night, so none of us slept well. We thought you would be sleeping in and wanted you to have as much rest as possible."

Which was so completely sweet and unsurprising of my mates.

Tilting my head back to look at the window, I arched a brow. "Wait, does this mean we have to skip class? I feel really restless, Jagger, and I'm worried if I stay in here all day I'm going to overthink last night. I know you usually like to avoid large gatherings when it's storming, but—"

Jagger's thumb ran over my lips as my rambling increased in speed, panicked at the idea of being stuck in my head all day. "Don't worry, we're going to class. We know how important it is to you, and the storms should be over now."

A sigh of relief left me.

"News of our meeting last night has already traveled through the sector, though. Linan tried to spread rumors through Fletcher's underlings after the meeting, trying to paint the picture of what happened, but luckily Thomas got to his brother first. Still, we should expect some blowback."

"Great," I mumbled, feeling more nervous than ever. 'Blowback' was probably a very light way to describe what we'd have to deal with.

"Don't worry, little treasure." Jagger kissed the center of my forehead, and a rumble from his dragon left his chest. "We're going to figure all of this out."

"I believe you." Of course I believed him—I trusted all of my mates completely.

I pulled back after savoring the touch, looking down at his lips. I let out a small whimper as he leaned forward and teased my bottom lip with a nip, causing a shiver to trail over my skin. I absolutely loved the way that Jagger seemed to take control in moments like this, when we were alone, and he proved my point in a single second when I found myself flat on my back on the bed.

"Jagger," I whispered as I deepened the kiss, his one hand tangling in my hair and tilting my head exactly how he wanted it, the other pushing up my shirt and resting on my bare waist.

"I love you underneath me," he growled, his voice filled with a heat that bathed me in desire and need all at once. I moved one leg up to his hip and tried to pull him further against me, a moan leaving my lips at the feeling of his hardness pressed right against my center.

"I love being here." I paused, not knowing if I should even say the rest but wanting to be honest with him. "I love being trapped underneath you."

Jagger stilled for a minute, pulling back and examining my face, his eyes darkening to almost a charcoal color. "Do you mean that, little treasure?"

"Yes." I swallowed nervously. "I don't fully understand it, but I love it. I like feeling like you're in control."

A nearly feral sound left Jagger's throat as he put his head down for a moment, seeming to be reaching for...control, maybe? I couldn't consider his reaction fully, though, because the sound he produced had my entire system lighting up as I forced myself to not rub against him.

"Jagger..." I whispered, close to begging him to move.

"On your stomach, little treasure."

A sense of nervous excitement filtered over me, heat saturating everything at the change that rolled over my mate. All of his tension and caution was gone, and instead a dominance radiated off of him. It was so incredibly hot that I felt almost dazed by it, completely captivated by the man.

I wanted Jagger. No, I *needed* Jagger.

"What?" I knew he'd asked me to do something, but I couldn't remember. It was hard for me to focus when I could see the outline of his cock in those sweats he was wearing.

"On your stomach. Now."

I didn't hesitate, turning over so that I was on my stomach facing away from him. In the process, my shirt bunched up, revealing the bottom of my lace panties. Jagger cursed as his rough fingers ran over the edge, and I fought the urge to push my butt back against his hand, knowing he wanted me to stay still.

I didn't want that though. I wanted all of his touch.

"Good girl." He leaned over me and nipped the top of my ear. "Now don't move unless I tell you. Understand?"

"Yes, Jagger," I whimpered, and he made a noise

that sounded so pleased that I spread my legs, knowing he was planning to touch me.

His fingers tightened on my skin. "Don't move." Then those fingers moved to the side of my panties, tugging them down and off in a quick movement. I shivered as his lips trailed up the back of my thigh, and when he tugged up my hips, I happily pressed my butt back, feeling completely exposed to him.

"Fuck," Jagger hissed, his fingers trailing over my wet heat and nearly causing me to jolt forward. "You're soaking my fingers already. Do you like this, little treasure? You like doing exactly what you're told like a good girl?"

Those words caused my entire body to tighten as I nodded, unable to answer, worried my voice would crack in excitement.

"Answer," he demanded softly, his fingers pausing.

"Yes, I love it.".

My eyes nearly rolled back as I was rewarded with two thick digits sliding inside of me, filling me in one pump. I couldn't help but spread my legs further, wanting more. I wanted to know what it felt like when each of my mates filled me. I wanted to know how it felt to be marked by them when they were deep inside of me.

"Greedy," he growled as I continued to push

back against him, his fingers filling me again and again. "You're so tight around my fingers; I can practically feel how much you need to come."

"I do," I whimpered, rocking against him.

"I won't make you suffer," Jagger rumbled. "I'm going to make you come all over my fingers before I lick it up. Then you're going to help me, little treasure—you're going to take that sweet mouth of yours and suck on my cock."

Oh shit.

I moaned his name, the only form of assent I was capable of giving at the moment. I loved how dirty he was talking, and I one hundred percent wanted to give him that and so much more.

"Words, little treasure." His fingers paused as I tightened around him.

"Yes, I promise." I moaned as he started pumping his fingers again, faster this time, causing me to nearly melt into the bed. When his thumb rolled over my clit, every ounce of pleasure surged forward and collapsed over me like a tidal wave.

I cried out his name as my entire body trembled with the relief of his touch. I whimpered, barely registering as his tongue ran the seam of my center, licking up my release. When he sucked on my clit, my eyes squeezed shut as another much smaller climax rolled over me.

Remembering my promise, I eagerly got on all fours and crawled over to where he stood at the edge of the bed. His gaze ran over me in satisfaction as he curled his finger, causing me to nearly scramble off the bed. I couldn't help the way my cheeks lit up as he put a pillow on the floor before tangling his fingers in my hair and kissing me, hard and possessive.

"Shirt off," he demanded, his voice soft but dangerous. "I want to see all of you while you're on your knees."

The growl that left his lips as I tugged my shirt off gave me an excited thrill. Switching places with my mate, I went down on my knees, my fingers running over the edge of his sweatpants before I met his gaze.

"Take me out, little treasure." He gripped my chin. "Take my cock out and put it between your perfect fucking lips."

Tugging down his sweats, I nearly trembled at the sight of how large he was, his cock impossibly hard with a drip of pre-cum on the tip. I didn't hesitate to surge forward and lick it off, causing his hand to go from my chin to my hair, the sensation a slight sting in the best way possible.

Wrapping my hand around the base of his length, I took his cock in my mouth, the salty taste causing my thighs to press together. The primal noise that left him, one of satisfaction and possessiveness, had me taking him as deep as possible. When I gagged slightly on his length, though, he absolutely lost it.

Relaxing my throat and mouth, he began to slide in and out between my lips, stroking himself and using my body for relief. Something I absolutely loved. The way he controlled everything, down to the hold he had on my head, was intoxicating. It felt like I had no power at all, and every single ounce of it at the same time. The fact that I could elicit this type of reaction from this man was absolutely insane, and it had me nearly climaxing on the spot.

"Touch yourself." His voice was so rough it barely sounded like him. "Rub that pussy until you come with me, Bex."

The desire to have him come down my throat was impossible to describe, so I did exactly what he demanded. I moved a hand to my center as I tried to even take him deeper, and his grip turned harder on me.

"Fuck," he growled. "Just like that. Shit, Bex—"

I whimpered as I rubbed my clit faster, and my climax came over me almost immediately. The sensation of him thrusting once more into my mouth before holding himself there, causing my eyes to nearly water, was one that I loved. I swallowed down his cum as molten pleasure coated my skin, satisfaction reigning supreme.

"Little treasure."

I blinked, looking up as Jagger's touch turned soft and he slowly pulled out of my mouth, staring at me in shock and what felt like a bit of awe. I made a pleased noise as he lifted me into his arms and kissed me hard, not caring that I had just swallowed down his release. I whispered his name as he sat down on the edge of the bed, keeping me in his lap, his bare cock pressed right against my center.

How was he still freakin' hard?

"That would be your fault," he rumbled, causing my toes to curl and my cheeks to flush. Apparently I'd said that out loud.

Before I could respond, a curse and crash sounded in the other room. My brows shot up as Gage appeared in the door, but instead of looking pissed, an almost antagonistic smile flitted to his lips as he held Jagger's gaze.

"And it's both of your faults—mainly his, cupcake—that Breaker just shifted and broke part of the bridge."

"What?!" I crawled off Jagger and grabbed a robe. Gage chuckled, kissing my temple as I rushed past him into the main room. I heard Jagger getting his pants back on behind me, but my focus was on the bridge railing that was broken.

"What happened?" I turned to look at Jagger and Gage.

"He's being dramatic." Gage flashed a smile. "Nice to *not* be the one out of control anymore, though."

"Only because I didn't touch your mark," Jagger leveled, causing the man to let out a dangerous rumble.

"No, seriously." I frowned and looked to the sky where Breaker's dragon soared. "What happened?"

"It's because it smells like your cum in here," Gage explained, chuckling. "His dragon lost it, wanting to mark you—and then that happened."

Well...he should have just joined us, then.

"Little treasure," Jagger groaned.

Gage chuckled roughly as my cheeks flushed... Well, clearly I had also said that out loud. I'd been doing that more often than before, it felt like...but I found I didn't regret it.

I meant it...I just didn't know if I was ready for more than one of them yet.

Chapter 5

Bexley Blackforge

"Breaker." I smiled as his lips pressed against my throat, my cheeks blushing at the image we made in the mirror. His massive frame overshadowed mine, and with only a robe on while getting ready, I couldn't help but imagine us in this exact position...but not getting ready for classes.

Fates. I swear, this sex drive was going to get the best of me. How was I supposed to focus when I had three sexy mates who seemed to always find me attractive? That was going to be a huge problem since it seemed we had a lot of important things to do.

"Yes, *mo chuisle?*"

I shook my head, smiling at the cute way his arm wrapped around my waist. Applying a little bit of mascara, having managed to get my hair and face in a presentable state for the day, I turned into him and tilted my head up.

"I was worried when you flew off, but now you seem...okay?" My fingers played with his hair as he let out a low rumble, which apparently was all the answer I was going to get. Instead he leaned forward and captured my freshly lipsticked lips before picking me up and burying his head against my neck again.

I let out a small giggle as he carried me from the room, feeling fairly refreshed after coffee, a shower, brushing my teeth, and getting ready. Although Jagger hadn't liked any of that because he complained about it removing his scent.

"Seriously?" Jagger asked, scowling as we passed. Breaker stopped and set me down to grab another cup of coffee for me, putting it in a travel mug and placing it near my bag.

"What?" I asked in confusion. Gage shook his head, his gaze resting on the other side of my neck—not the side Breaker was on—before seeming to relax. Then Breaker picked me back up and carried me into my room, closing the door behind us.

I heard the muffled conversation of the others, but Breaker soon had all my attention as he set me on the bed and went to my closet.

"What do you want to wear?" he asked. His tone was light, but there was something up with Breaker right now, an energy to him that wasn't usually there.

"Um..." I stood and walked towards the closet, glad that despite it being gloomy, the actual rain had stopped. Apparently it would be stormy on and off today, but nothing we couldn't handle for class. At least that was what my mates continued to assure me.

"Oh, I haven't worn this yet!" I grabbed a pastel pink tulle skirt that was mid length, falling to my calf, and a thin white sweater, happily handing both to Breaker when he offered a hand. Then I went in search of one of my favorite gold belts and a scarf that had pink and gold in it as well. It was one of those square silk ones that could be worn on your neck or head and look equally as fabulous. After finding a pair of white boots and my trench coat, I turned to find Breaker holding my clothes against his nose, his eyes closed—

"Are you smelling my clothes?" He totally was, and it was actually pretty adorable.

Breaker's eyes opened, and the tips of his ears turned pink. "Yes," he admitted in a low rumble.

"He's also scenting them!" Jagger called through the door. "Bastard." That last part was mumbled, though. A cocky smile pressed onto Breaker's lips, and he shrugged unapologetically.

"I like your scent," I said. Breaker placed my clothes on the bed before surging forward and lifting me up to give me a tentative, sweet kiss.

"Good, because I've been covering you in it all morning."

Unable to *not* love the idea of being covered in his scent, I watched happily as he left my room to join the others. I knew Jagger didn't like the idea of his scent being covered—heck, I don't think any of them liked it—but considering how worked up Breaker had been, I felt better knowing he was more content with the situation now.

Getting dressed quickly, I turned in the mirror and secured the scarf around my neck in a neat fold before walking out to the main room and shrugging on my trench.

"I like that color on you," Jagger said, handing me my travel mug. He and the others were ready for class as well.

"Thank you. I love pink—I actually love most pastel colors."

"Her purse collection speaks for itself," Gage agreed, making me narrow my eyes. I knew exactly how he felt about my purses. Or at least how he said he felt about them...

"Gage thinks I have too many purses," I announced, his eyes shooting up and filling with mirth.

"I *know* you have too many," he mused.

"I do not," I scoffed.

"I think you should have as many as you want," Breaker said, causing me to smile softly at the sweet statement. I probably did have too many, though.

"How many?" Jagger asked curiously.

"Over fifty."

He nearly spit out his coffee as Breaker let out a low whistle. I scowled at Gage as his smile grew. "That's not even the crazy part! The crazy part is how much the damn things cost. A car I can understand, but a purse? A tiny piece of leather or whatever the hell they're made out of? I just can't see it."

"It's not that bad!" I squeaked. "I only own ten that I would classify as 'car' level, and your mom was the one that imported them. I just picked which ones I liked!"

They were from the human plane and so incredibly pretty...

"Two hundred and seventy-three thousand." Gage smirked. "That's how much one of them was in Earth currency, and I remember the price because the bag was this teeny tiny piece of gold leather, like a box."

"Holy shit." Breaker chuckled before assuring me, "I'm sure it was worth it though."

"It's beautiful! It's literally beautiful, and I had no idea it was so much, Gage—you didn't even tell me until now!"

"Of course I didn't." Gage mused. "It doesn't matter. I was just surprised."

"You have amazing taste. I'm sure it was perfect," Jagger said. "Don't listen to him. You should be able to have ten of those each year if you want."

"Oh, she can have them, but it doesn't mean I won't say shit," Gage mused, loving every moment of this.

Leaning into Jagger, I narrowed my eyes playfully. "Well, I guess I should return it..."

"No." Gage looked offended. "Absolutely not."

I offered Jagger and Breaker a small smile and shrugged. "If you insist."

"Return it," Gage mocked, shaking his head. "Come on, let's go to class before you decide to return everything we've bought you."

"I won't return anything," I promised, fixing my sleeve and smiling to myself. I momentarily paused on my gorgeous dragon bracelet, the metallic shades representing me and my three mates so perfectly... which of course I realized now was on purpose.

Gage could complain all he wanted, but the real

person who had a shopping problem here *was not me*.

During our quick walk to the main campus, I told the three of them about my dream, keeping my voice quiet. I knew we couldn't fully discuss it right now, but being able to tell them made me feel a bit better—like I wasn't going to spend the rest of my day overthinking it.

"We can talk about it more on the way to your old territory, but I think we should look into it," Gage said.

"Especially since it was directed at you and seems to fit your life pretty damn perfectly," Breaker agreed.

"Wait." I paused on the path right before we reached the main academic building, Jagger's hand sliding over my hip. "Are we going? I know you said you were going to make plans..."

"I talked to Estrid," Gage said, "and we can go after class. It may mean missing Monday depending how long we're gone, though, and I know that you don't want to miss any more classes."

"It's Friday, it should be enough time..." I hesitated. "But I want to go there no matter what. I know we've been traveling a lot, but I also think that maybe I need to accept that my time at DIA won't be normal. This situation won't rest, especially if Clanguard is willing to come here."

"If that's what you want, then we'll go," Jagger assured me.

I looked at all three of my mates and nodded. "I want it handled more than anything."

"Maybe if we don't spend too much time there we can also stop in the city," Breaker said as we resumed walking.

"Wouldn't be a bad thing," Gage agreed. "I haven't brought it up to my parents yet, but I feel like it may be better handled ourselves."

I didn't know what to think about that. The idea of going into the city made me uncomfortable, but I also knew that it was somewhat unavoidable. If Clanguard was spreading rumors here, I couldn't imagine what he was saying back home.

"During the course of this next week, I want you to research one of the prominent families within Trabea," our professor Mrs. Meeker said while passing out packets that would accompany our normal reading. "It can be one of the dragon clans or any of the city communities—just has to be prominent enough that you can find information on them."

"Who are you going to do?" Rachel asked, writing quickly in her notebook as we received the packet in the back row. Despite the rumors that were flying around judging by the looks I kept getting, Rachel hadn't acted any differently towards me when I'd made it to class and slipped in right behind her—both of us late.

I'd been so caught up on saying goodbye to each of my mates that I hadn't realized the courtyard had cleared and classes were about to start. Well, until I saw my friend's pink hair as she ran towards class. I wouldn't lie, it made me feel a bit better that I wasn't the only one bad with time.

Although Rachel was normally really good with schedules, from what I could tell. I had a feeling something was going on because she not only looked exhausted, but her eyes looked just the tiniest bit puffy, like she'd been crying.

"Not the Flash Clan for sure; not after last night," I mumbled. Rachel's eyes lit with a bit of humor and sympathy, squeezing my hand. Clearly, Professor Clanguard had told her what was going on. That was a relief—I was worried she hadn't treated me differently because she just hadn't known.

"Who cares what they think," she said. "Seriously, Bex. Aside from the fact that you're literally at the top of the pyramid here, trying to get their approval is exhausting."

There was the hint of sadness again.

"You aren't wrong...I'm just tired of all the looks. I don't want to be scary, I just want to be...normal, I guess?" I shook my head. "It's not even about that, though, because before I was a shifter who hadn't shifted. I guess I don't like the idea of people thinking I'm willing to hurt those around me."

"Anyone who knows you knows you would never," Rachel said before relaxing back into her chair. "Plus, those assumptions are usually a reflection of people's own thoughts on the system. I know I would have thought the same without knowing you because I'm used to predators acting like that. Now I know better."

"Because of your mates also," I added, completely tuning out whatever the teacher was saying. I think she was answering questions from the class.

"One of them," Rachel drew out, her brow dipping. "Not Fletcher, that's for sure."

"Something happen?"

Rachel's eyes darkened, making me regret asking. I didn't want her to be upset.

"Yeah you could say that," she muttered. "We

had plans for dinner and he stood me up. I know his family is here, and I can't say I'm surprised, but...it just sucked. It's bullcrap."

My jaw tightened, feeling a surge of anger towards the wolf alpha. "That is bullcrap. Have you seen him today?"

"Nope." She closed her notebook. "And I don't want to."

"Excuse me, Mrs. Meeker?" The loud voice brought me back to the present, and I realized that people were starting to pack up.

"Yes?" she asked.

"Can we do families that aren't prominent but were?"

I froze, narrowing my eyes at the group of people who used to hang around Ioan. I tried to school my reaction as Rachel let out a small defensive growl that surprised me.

"Like who?" Mrs. Meeker asked cautiously.

"Like the Blackforge family, from the Flash Clan," the girl said easily.

Shaking my head, I ignored the jab and packed up my stuff, not bothering to listen to Mrs. Meeker's answer. Rachel had her stuff ready by the time I stood up and walked out the door. It wasn't worth the fight, and I knew the girl was trying to insult me by saying my family wasn't 'prominent,' which really didn't matter to me. However, if she got up in front of the class and started to talk bad about them—

"Bex." Rachel pulled me to a stop, and I looked down at where she'd grabbed me, noticing gold smoke rolling over my fingers. I shook my hand and frowned, taking a deep, calming breath.

"They're assholes," Rachel insisted.

I nodded but deflated. "It just makes me not want to go to class."

"I'm sure Mrs. Meeker will shut that down," she stated.

I hoped so.

"Rachel."

As we entered the main hall and walked towards the lunch room to find my mates, I heard Fletcher's voice echo through the space. I didn't stop, though, following my friend's lead. Her jaw tightened, but other than that she didn't react.

As we made it through the door and into the main dining hall, his voice turned slightly louder. "Rachel!"

She kept walking.

"Damnit—Rachel."

This time everyone in the hall went quiet as my friend came to a stop. She offered me a carefully concealed expression, her sadness barely present, before turning to face her mate. I stood silently next to her, wanting her to know I supported her. Although I wouldn't lie, seeing Fletcher made me angry. Mainly because of what he was putting my friend through, but also because he looked so much like Linan.

"Yes, Fletcher?"

The future alpha finally noticed everyone in the room staring, but he didn't retreat, keeping his eyes on his mate. "We need to talk. Now."

"Then talk," Rachel said evenly.

"In private. Alone," he gritted out.

Her smile turned sad. "No. I'm not going to play this game. It's bad enough that I feel like my own mate doesn't want anyone to know we're together—"

Whispers started up, and I saw concern flash in Fletcher's gaze. I had a feeling what this was about, and it didn't negate Rachel's feelings about the situation—even if he was trying to protect her.

"But to be stood up for a simple dinner? No. I may be a prey shifter, Fletcher, but I am not going to let you play around with my feelings. You know we're mates, and you knew how I felt about you—"

"*Felt?*"

Rachel swallowed, emotion flooding her gaze as she shrugged. "I can't wait forever. I...I want you to leave me alone."

Actual panic infused Fletcher's gaze, and when Rachel went to step back, he lunged forward—

A flash of a body intercepted and slammed into him. My brows shot up as I took in Fletcher on the ground with Diane standing over him, a smug smile on her face. Sue, her sidekick, appeared next to us and offered me a head nod. I had no idea if we were on good terms, but I also didn't really get their entire dynamic.

"She said leave her alone." Diane stepped towards us, her eyes narrowing. "Your *mate* wants you to leave her alone—so leave her alone."

"None of you are part of this," Fletcher said, trying to keep the growl out of his voice.

"That's not true." Diane's face turned far more serious. "In fact, I would say I am very much part of this, especially if I need to protect her...which considering who you are, I may need to do just that. After all, we share the same horrible father. Don't we, brother?"

What?

I reared back as Diane arched a brow at Fletcher, his face turning pale.

"Maybe we should talk about this outside," I said evenly, instinctively knowing that this was about to dive into somewhere a lot darker.

Before they could respond, though, I felt my

mates enter the room, and Breaker's booming voice filled the space. "Everyone out. Now."

They definitely listened, all of the other students scrambling from their seats.

I stared in surprise at the two alphas— *Fletcher was Diane's brother?*—as I kept a supportive hand on Rachel's back, her face impossibly sad. Sue was pacing, and Diane was having a stare-off with Fletcher, who looked almost sick. I offered my mates a concerned look as they spread throughout the room. I was glad they weren't trying to stop this, instead making sure everyone involved had the privacy they deserved.

"What do you mean?" Fletcher finally demanded.

"I mean that until yesterday I had no idea that the man who visited my mother time and time again, resulting in not just me but four of my sisters—not willingly, mind you—was your daddy dearest. I also didn't realize he was the Alpha of the Clanguard pack, but damn does that make a lot of fucking sense. Entitled pieces of shit."

I let out a sharp exhale as I looked between them, seeing the subtle similarities. Fletcher blinked and ran a hand over his face, not looking surprised, exactly...but there was something there, some extreme emotion. "My father forced your mom into mating?"

"Yes. Produced five girls. He hated that." She smirked, but the expression was the opposite of joyful. "He came by to tell me to tell my mother hello. Isn't that fucking sweet of him?"

"Bastard," I thought I heard Gage mutter. I didn't disagree with him in the least.

"I don't know what to say to that," Fletched growled, looking frustrated. "He's a piece of shit, but that has nothing to do with Rachel and me."

"It is if your mate wants nothing to do with you and you won't leave her alone," Diane spit out. "Apple doesn't fall far from the tree."

"Diane," I said, treading carefully. "I think that may be a bit extreme—"

"Extreme?" Diane spun on me, causing Jagger to stand defensively, but he didn't move forward. "*Extreme* is hearing your mom sob herself to sleep every time your biological father comes to visit her. *Extreme* is knowing that you and your sisters were not only unwanted but a product of forced mating. That is *extreme*."

"I'm nothing like my father." Fletcher's words were heavy, saturated with power and anger. "The entire fucking reason I'm trying to keep Rachel away is because of that. Until the bastard is dead, there's nothing I can do to change the pack dynamic, so I'm trying my damn best to keep her out of his sight line."

As sad as it was, his explanation made sense. Diane seemed to be thinking along the same lines as she looked down at Rachel, who was staring at her mate with caution. "Have you explained that to her?"

His silence spoke volumes. Taking a step back into Gage's arms, I let out a shaky breath, not knowing how to feel about any of this.

"Can we talk? Alone?" Fletcher asked. Rachel took a long moment before nodding, and I watched in surprise as she took his hand and they walked out towards the large doors, leaving my three mates and the two girls behind.

"Follow them. They should be fine, but just in case," Diane told Sue before turning towards me, offering me a clinical look. "You didn't step in."

"It was a conversation, not a fight. I had a guess why Fletcher was doing what he was doing, even if I didn't agree with it—still don't," I admitted. "Linan Clanguard is...I know what a problem he is, to say the least."

Diane's eyes filled with sadness. "Keep an eye on your friend, Bexley. I don't trust any of Fletcher's underlings, especially now that Walker is gone."

What? "Walker's gone?"

My mates stilled, and Diane offered us a cynical laugh as she made her way towards the door. "Something like that."

The minute the doors closed, leaving the four of us alone, I turned towards my mates. "That was....intense."

"To say the least," Jagger agreed. "Are you okay, little treasure?"

"I will be. What happened with Walker?"

"He was removed from campus," Breaker said.

I was glad he was gone, but this was the second person I was responsible for being kicked out...

"Don't overthink it." Gage kissed my ear. "They'll figure their shit out, and we're always going to keep you safe, which means kicking assholes out if they fuck with you."

"You say it like it's so simple," I mumbled.

"Because it is."

"Come on, little treasure." Jagger nodded towards the door. "Let's get ready to visit the rogue lands. The sooner we leave, the sooner we can come back."

Allowing him to lead me away, I couldn't help but worry over the idea of me getting two students kicked out.

Was I the true problem here?

Chapter 6

Breaker Firespell

Damn this sector's rapid changes in weather. I tucked *mo chuisle's* jacket around her, the cooler autumn air making me concerned as we stepped out of the elevator, bags in hand. "Do you want to run up and get a heavier jacket?"

"It feels good," she promised me, her eyes filled with a warmth that I would never fully get used to. After looking her over, glad she'd changed into a pair of jeans and a sweater, I nodded and placed a hand around her waist as we walked forward. Jagger and Gage were already waiting on the path ahead, having come down here a few minutes ago.

While I knew it was necessary, I wasn't a huge fan of leaving the sector—more specifically our dorm. Not only did Bexley love the handcrafted space, but

I was comfortable in it, and I knew it like the back of my hand. Where we were going now...well, I barely fucking remembered the place.

Although my memories with Bexley while visiting her were crystal clear, I had never taken much interest in the Flash Clan's lands. I only knew that they were beautiful and had a mountainous terrain, creating a natural defensive barrier. I nearly shook my head at that, exhausted by the fact that my brain always slipped into a more logistical and military-focused way of thinking.

I hoped that once I moved away from my parents for good and spent more time around the softness that Bexley infused in everything, that it would fade. Although even I could admit it went a long way to making me feel as though I could protect her fully...

Still, as we walked down the path, her mood much lighter than it'd been in the dining hall, I remembered one of many instances when Bexley's sweet attitude had altered my outlook on things.

"Again." A grunt left my lips at my father's command as one of his soldiers ran towards me with a sparring sword in hand. I easily maneuvered my way around the man, and in seconds my own sword was jabbing into his chest. My father clapped in approval—a

singular clap, but it was enough to make me feel proud.

"Good job, Breaker. Let's go again—"

For fates' sake. Hours. We had been at this for hours.

"Breaker!"

Excitement surged through me like a lightning bolt as Bexley's voice rang across the training yard. I heard my father curse under his breath as all his soldiers knelt in a sign of respect, her gaze fully on me and barely noticing. I knew my father didn't like being interrupted, but he'd also been the one to invite the Blackforge family here for a visit.

"Morning, Bex." I offered her a smile and used my shirt to wipe off my face, which was covered in sweat. I felt a stab of insecurity because I knew I probably looked bad. It wasn't something I thought about a lot, except around my friend. Then again, it didn't matter that it was early morning—training having started at dawn—Bexley looked so incredibly pretty that it made my chest hurt.

That thought had me wondering if other people noticed that—noticed her. I tried to shake that thought and the sudden urge to bring her inside and hang out there. I didn't like the idea of all the other soldiers out here seeing her, some of them in training and as young as we were.

"Bexley," my father said in greeting. "I didn't realize you would be up so early."

Bex offered my dad a bright smile and tilted her head, looking around. "How could I not be? I barely get time to see Breaker, and he told me he had a ton of fun things planned for us."

She wasn't wrong. I'd spent the entire week making plans.

"Is that so?" My father's lips pressed up into what I would nearly call a smile before he met my gaze. I thought I would see disappointment there, but instead I saw something like understanding. "Well, he's been training for hours now, so I think he's good to go. Breaker, do you want to practice anymore?"

"Nope." I gave him a thankful head nod and led Bexley towards the estate. "See you at dinner, Dad!"

He chuckled as I led her towards the large doors of the estate and listened to her tell me all about a dream she had. I barely remembered her actual words, though. Instead I was captivated by two things.

First, the relief I felt at having her out of the line of sight of every male out there. It wasn't something I understood, but my instincts were rarely wrong when it came to my friends. More importantly, Bexley.

Secondly, the fact that just by her mere presence, she had completely altered my morning—hell, my entire day. Only Bex could do that.

. . .

"Breaker." Bexley's lips forming my name had me looking down at her, realizing that I'd zoned out for most of our walk towards the gate into the academy's central pavilion. The other two were talking, but my mate was completely focused on me.

"Sorry." I chuckled softly. "I was reliving a memory I'd sort of forgotten."

"Oh? About what?"

"Your family had come to visit and I was stuck training all morning, but you woke up early just to hang out with me all day. Made my fucking day," I admitted easily. Her eyes lit up, making me happy that I'd decided to tell her.

"I love that." She squeezed my hand. "I also completely believe it. I hope I get that memory back as well."

"You will," I said firmly. There was no way she wouldn't. I wished it was as easy as giving her all my memories so she could see every moment like I did. To remember every single time that we were together and the impact it made on me.

"We good?" Gage asked, looking back and waiting for confirmation before we stepped through the gate.

As soon as we were through, the cooler weather

neutralized, and I found myself shaking my head. I wasn't sure I would ever fully get used to the magic at this school. Of course I knew there were magic users of all kinds, but this brand of magic still baffled me to an extent.

"Headmistress Estrid should be out soon," Jagger assured Bexley as she looked around at the other sector gates with curiosity.

She turned to face us, hope reflected in her gold gaze. "I hope when all of this is done we get to visit the other sectors...maybe even territories. I feel like there's so much separation."

I took a deep breath, knowing the others wouldn't agree with what I was about to say because honestly it was fucking dangerous to traverse the other territories. "If you want to go, we will make it happen, Bex."

"Even the witch territory?" she teased, looking at the other two.

"No fucking way," Jagger muttered, then offered a compromise. "How about one of the others?"

"Fae? Vampires? Demi-gods?" Bexley teased.

"All of them are so fucking bad," Gage grunted.

"You think everyone who isn't one of you three is bad." She let out an amused hum as she leaned into me. "I think we should visit all of them, because I know if I'm with you three, I'm safe."

And fuck did I love that she believed and trusted in us that much.

When the pair of doors to the administration building swung open, Estrid made her way down the steps, offering us a pleasant smile. "I apologize for the delay; I was caught up in some paperwork." The headmistress seemed far less stressed than she'd been a few days ago—although she may have just been hiding it. "Paperwork is a nasty thing, isn't it?"

"The worst," Bexley said, causing me to smile. My mate wasn't the type to sit for long periods of time. She was always up and moving around, so the idea of sitting in an office doing paperwork undoubtedly bored her.

"How have things been?" Estrid asked as she led us towards the portal. "Already your first two weeks have been riddled with problems. I hope it doesn't reflect too poorly on us."

"I don't think it's a reflection of the school at all," Bexley said. "I think that life happens, and how you react to it is what matters."

Estrid squeezed her shoulder. "Wonderfully said."

Before she opened the portal, she turned to face all of us, her expression growing somber. "On that note, I was made aware of what happened last night by Professor Clanguard. When I allowed the families in, I assumed it was for a simple visit, not an interrogation. DIA is your home, and you are not subject to their questions unless you are okay with that. Understand?"

"We appreciate that," Jagger said. His tone was even, but I could tell from the tension in his frame that he was still upset about yesterday, and I didn't blame him.

"Most of them behaved," Gage assured her, "but there were a few individuals who shouldn't be allowed on campus in general, and not just because of our situation."

Like fucking Clanguard.

"And we plan to handle them outside of the walls of DIA from now on," I pointed out, trying to keep my threat veiled. Though I was pretty sure I'd failed when I saw the small smile that pulled at her lips.

"Very good then." She clapped happily and her magic easily exploded out, creating a portal that would transport us right into our territory.

"Thank you for this," Bexley said sweetly as Estrid ushered us through. I wrapped my arm around Bexley before throwing our weight into the portal, keeping her secure to me.

It was better to get this shit out of the way.

As the cold air saturated down to my bones, I

tried to only focus on the feeling of her being in my arms instead of the annoying thump in my head. I hated portalling. I didn't hate many things, but this was bullshit and I never felt right after doing it, at least for a solid twenty-four hours.

All at once, though, it was over.

I groaned as I stumbled out of the portal onto a grassy hill with Bex still in my arms. I had to stop my momentum before barreling into the car waiting for us, and Bexley let out a squeak as I turned sharply so that my back would take the brunt of the impact.

The car shifted as we slammed into it, and I winced, knowing that it would leave a dent.

"Holy crap!" Bexley let out a surprised giggle. "Did you almost tip over that car?"

"Maybe." I grunted, hating that the world felt like it was built of damn cardboard sometimes. Before I had to give a definitive answer, though, the other two were making their way through the portal, both catching themselves far easier than I had. Bastards.

"Everything good?" Gage asked, then took a closer look at the car. "Shit, did you dent that?"

"Shut it," I muttered. Jagger chuckled, grabbing the keys from the wheel well and unlocking the SUV before tossing them to Gage. Normally I would have offered to drive, but I was a needy bastard today and felt a surge of relief when Jagger sat up front to keep him company. I wanted to not only have Bex to myself but to keep her thoughts occupied as we made our way to what used to be her home.

Not anymore, though, and not just because of her past.

No, her home was with us now.

"It feels weird being back in the territory but not going home," she said, tilting her head so she was looking up at me. My arm was around her as she leaned into my side, giving me the contact I craved. "Well, I suppose it's not my home anymore..."

"Where do you want to live, *mo chuisle*?"

"I don't know. I don't like the idea of being too far from everyone we know, but I also think it would be weird if we just picked one clan territory to stay in, you know?"

"I do." I brushed my lips against her temple, an idea forming. "Maybe you'll like the rogue lands. Hell, I can't call it that anymore, can I? Maybe you'll end up loving the Flash Clan lands and want to move there."

"That's not a bad idea." She nibbled her lip. "I do worry about the memories, though."

"We have all the time in the world. No rush," I said, wanting to take away her worry. "We'll go wherever you go."

"Yeah?" she whispered, her fingers reaching up to brush over the mark she'd given me. I immediately tugged her onto my lap. I'd been wanting to this entire time, but there was no way she could touch me like that and I wouldn't react.

"Yes." I cupped her jaw gently. "You know I would do anything for you, *mo chuisle*."

"*Mo chuisle*." Bexley mulled over the nickname, her fingers playing over my pulse and her mark. "You said it means 'my pulse,' right? Is that how you really think of me?"

I'd told Bexley I loved her, but I knew she needed to know how deeply important her existence in my life was—because it went past love.

"Do I think of you like that?" I repeated, trying to find the right words. "Bexley...you are everything to me. You are the reason my heart beats, for the blood running through my veins. So yes, *mo chuisle,* you are my very pulse—essential to my very being."

Bexley's eyes watered, a look of pure joy filtered across her face. "Breaker, I love you. I love you so much."

Pressing forward and kissing her softly, savoring the touch, I let out a low rumble. "I love you too, Bexley."

I needed her to know that she had all of me—that

no matter what she wanted, what she decided—the most important factor was *her*.

My arms wrapped tightly around her as the car began to climb in altitude, knowing that when we got to her estate she'd be flooded with so many emotions, and not all of them good. I could see the structure in the distance as we passed the border into her lands, looking more like a castle than a simple estate.

With a deep inhale, Bexley kissed my cheek and turned to face her old home—her past.

Chapter 7

Bexley Blackforge

"That...that's it? That's my old home?" My voice was a bit wobbly as I stared at the castle in the distance.

I hadn't known what to expect from the Rogue lands—all I knew was that they rested on the most southern border of all three clan territories, similar to how the city rested to the north. I had no idea it would be like *this*, though—this absolutely stunning landscape.

From the moment we passed through an ivy-covered archway made of stone and drove down a paved road that trailed upwards through the mountains, towards the castle in question, I found myself in awe of our surroundings. Thick lush greenery rustled in the wind, sunlight highlighting the wild, unkempt landscape to each side. It hadn't invaded the road though, staying to the sides as if nature itself was trying to preserve my family's heritage.

"Your parents tried to maintain the natural surroundings of their territory as much as possible," Jagger said as if reading my mind. "At least that's what the book said when it talked about how the Flash Clan structured their lands."

"I like that," I said, my eyes catching sight of a form darting through the shadowed woods. I had a feeling there was a lot of wildlife around here, but I also had to assume it was called the 'rogue' lands for a reason. Right?

"This is going to seem silly." I sighed as I spoke a bit louder so the other two could hear me. "But why is it called the rogue lands? I feel like I should've learned about this in tutoring, but I can't remember."

"You didn't learn about it," Gage said. "Every time we brought up the rogue lands, especially on the map, it caused you so much pain that we stopped trying."

Oh. I had to wonder what else fell into that same category—what other information I was missing.

"The Rogue lands are similar to the city in the sense that there is no clan affiliation, but different because there is no formal community," Breaker explained. "At least as far as we know. If there is one, it isn't sectioned out like the city is by 'water shifter' or 'wolf shifter'—it would just be all of them together. At least that's our guess. We've left them to their own devices for some time now."

"They never cause problems, so no reason to interfere," Jagger added.

"It's never bothered any of your families that shifters choose not to live under your protection?" I asked.

"Never," Gage said with surety.

"I'm sure it bothers mine," Breaker said, "but they're overcontrolling, so that makes sense."

"I'm not sure, actually," Jagger admitted. "Then again, my parents tend to be pretty reserved about that type of thing."

Reflecting back on all my interactions with their parents and what the guys said about them, I was learning that the three of their families could not have been more different. It wasn't in a bad way, but it made me wonder how these men became so close when they were all raised in such different environments.

Before I could ask any more questions, Gage cursed and we came to a hard stop. Two men and one woman stood in the middle of the road, arms crossed and looking intimidating.

Well, sort of. It was hard to view much as intimidating when I had the mates that I had. I shifted off

Breaker's lap, reaching for the door handle. Better to ask them why they were stopping us instead of continuing this weird stare-off.

"Nope." Breaker's arm tightened around my waist, keeping me on his lap. Despite his secure hold on me, he didn't seem concerned. In fact, none of my mates seemed very concerned—so why the heck wasn't I allowed to get out?

Breaker pressed a kiss under my ear. "We don't know what threat they pose."

"Fine, fine," I murmured, "but someone has to get out."

Now it was Jagger who was reaching for the door handle. "Roll down the windows but keep the car running," he told Gage before he stepped out of the car, straightening to full height. His stance was relaxed and confident.

"We're just passing through to the old Flash Clan estate," he said easily. "We aren't looking for a problem."

The woman narrowed her eyes at him. "I'm aware why you're here, Silvershade."

Oh crap. Breaker made a surprised noise at the malice in her voice, and a sliver of unease trickled down my spine.

"Maybe he should—"

"I don't like the three heirs coming into our

land," she said darkly, her eyes moving to the car. "But our seer also said you're transporting Bexley Blackforge. Is that true?"

"Why does it matter?" Gage growled, but they couldn't hear him, so Jagger repeated the question. I was curious as well. Would my presence change her anger at my mates? A defensive energy filtered through my chest at the idea of anyone bearing ill will towards them, especially strangers—ones that seemed powerful, even from here.

"Why does it matter?" The woman stared at him like he was dense, causing an angry noise to leave my throat. Breaker soothed my back with a rough hand, but it wasn't helping. "It matters because only Blackforge is allowed through. She has business here; you do not."

I couldn't take any more. I tapped Breaker's arm, and he inhaled sharply but loosened his grip on me. Gage wasn't happy, but I slid out of the car, the woman's gaze immediately focusing on me.

"I do have business here, and so do my mates," I said evenly, trying to keep my voice soft. The woman seemed to become less aggressive now that she had eyes on me, but she was still holding her defensive posture.

"Bexley, it's nice to meet you. I'm Aurora." The

woman's smile was tight. "Our seer said you'd be coming."

"We just need to get into the estate," I said simply. "I'm trying to jog my memory—"

"She also said you would ruin our community. Sorry about this."

All at once, before I could even blink, everything exploded into action.

The car rocked and bodies flooded out from the forest, and I let out a surprised noise as Jagger pressed me back against the vehicle. Before anyone could get within five feet of us, Jagger's magic exploded out in silver flames that surrounded our car in a bubble. I saw the shifters stumble back as I took a shaky breath and looked up at my mate.

"Get in the car, little treasure," he said softly. I could practically feel his fury. My stomach dropped, knowing that this was going to end in violence if I didn't involve myself. Already I could hear the door on Gage's side opening. Crap.

"Hold on." I pressed a hand to his chest and raised my voice. "Aurora! You don't want to do this!"

"I have to do this!" she called back, her voice rising above the sounds of fear and panic outside of the bubble. "We've worked for years to create a community. I won't let you ruin it."

"I am not ruining it. I have no intention of

ruining anything. I'm just trying to remember what happened to my family!"

No answer came. Instead, the shifters regrouped and tried to surge forward *into* the warded bubble, Jagger's magic pushing them away in a silver electric burst. Bloodcurdling screams left their throats, and I could hear the anger growing.

"In the car, now," Gage said as he stepped out of the car, and Breaker opened the door and tugged me inside.

"Breaker, I don't want them hurt."

"They want to hurt you," he argued, gently holding my jaw so I couldn't look around. "They're going to knock them out, not kill them. I want you to tuck your head against my shoulder though, okay?"

"Wait, why—"

A boom of thunder echoed from above, and I jolted as Jagger and Gage's power collided in an explosion of bronze and silver that came down from the heavens themselves. I screamed as the car shuddered and the skies outside turned black. The flames disappeared and the fifty-something individuals around the car tried to surge forward—

A blast of power hit the crowd, and all around us they fell unconscious. Only Aurora was left standing, her face filled with shock and fear.

Breaking out of Breaker's hold, I scrambled out

the door, and he didn't try to stop me. I made a panicked noise, moving past my mates to kneel next to a young woman that looked far too pale. I put my fingers against her pulse and watched her inhale and exhale slowly before I was able to fully relax.

"I—" Aurora's words were cut off.

"If you ever put my mate in danger again, all of you will be dead," Gage warned, staring at the woman with a darkness that sent chills across my skin. I felt...torn. I loved how protective he was, but these people were just trying to protect their home.

"Aurora," I said, standing and stepping in front of my mates. "I am being completely serious. I am not here to destroy the rogue lands."

Her dark eyes filled with a modicum of hope, but sadness was painted across the rest of her face as she looked around. "It...it doesn't matter, does it? We couldn't stop you even if we wanted to."

Moving closer, I realized she was a wolf shifter—specifically an alpha—and nearly as young as myself, maybe a few years older. The weight on her shoulders made her appear far older than that, though.

"I lost my memory," I explained, stopping a few feet away from her and putting my hands out to show I had nothing to hide. "That is the reason I'm here."

"These were your family's lands," she spit out as

her face contorted with bitterness, looking back at the estate. "It would make sense for you to want them."

"I don't know what I want," I said honestly. "Of course the estate holds some connection to me, but I would never force you from your home. I'm not looking to disrupt anything, I'm just looking to remember. Remember my family. Remember what happened to them."

After a long moment of staring at me with cautious speculation, she inhaled and looked around. "How long will they be out?"

"Maybe an hour," Breaker said.

I couldn't help but love that they were letting me handle this. I could feel their concern through our mating bond, and I knew their instinct was to throw me into the car, but they stayed behind me, controlling the urge to steal me away.

I turned to check on them, and I couldn't help but appreciate how intense and striking they looked in this moment, their massive profiles silhouetted against the black skies above, as if their power was threatening to strike at any moment. It sent an exhilarating thrill over my skin, and I couldn't help but feel sort of possessive over the idea of Aurora seeing them. I turned back and found her watching me as if they didn't even exist, and my dragon calmed down a tiny bit.

"I just want to see the estate," I said, letting some of my raw insecurity slip through. "I just want to remember how my parents died so I know who to blame."

Realization filled her gaze, and she let out a long exhale. "Fine, I get it. I'm going to shift and run ahead. This...this is most of our people. The rest are children and older individuals, not threats. Please don't hurt them."

"If they don't attack, we have no need to," Jagger said.

Aurora nodded, and I backed up as she shifted into a gorgeous red wolf that sprinted away from us without a backward glance. I could smell her fear, and I felt bad about scaring her...until I turned and saw all of the bodies surrounding the car. Individuals who'd planned on hurting my mates at her instruction.

I didn't feel quite so bad after that.

"Let's go, cupcake," Gage said. "I don't trust them not to attack again once they wake up."

I made my way back to the car as Jagger and Breaker moved bodies out of the way. Above, the sky began to lighten, and when I got into the vehicle I asked a question that had been on the top of mind.

"Have you guys had to do that a lot?"

"The power collision?" Jagger asked, and I nodded.

"Yes," Gage said as he put the car into drive. "Mostly in training though, unless we're dealing with issues in the city or from another sector. Things have been fairly peaceful."

"In our territories, at least," Breaker agreed.

"That's what they expect, though. That's why people live in Storm Dragon territory," Jagger pointed out. "We were placed in charge to keep that level of peace for everyone."

That put a heavy responsibility on them, but it was worth it if it meant that so many families got to enjoy life in a safe and relaxed territory.

"I also have a feeling that the reason Aurora was so upset is because they've built something similar here," Gage said.

"I would never take that from them."

"We know." Breaker brushed his lips against my temple. "But they don't know that."

"But if we ever wanted to live in your old estate, I'm sure that is exactly what it would feel like to them, especially if shifters are living in it already."

Crap. I hadn't considered that. I guess I'd just assumed that the rogue lands surrounded it and the castle was left...empty? But that didn't make sense. It was probably a lot more fortified and safer than the houses in the territory. Why *wouldn't* they want to live there?

Especially since it was so beautiful. Warm sunstone and large towers that created a fairytale-like castle were surrounded by wild plant life that complemented the structure rather than over-whelmed it. I couldn't see past the high wall that surrounded it, my only visual path through an empty space where gates had once been, but now I under-stood why Aurora had been so worked up.

They were worried about me taking back my estate because they *all* lived there. They'd made it into a village.

Chapter 8

Bexley Blackforge

Our car slowly pulled through the gates, although it was really more of an arch-way. The sunstone entrance was covered in greenery like the one that'd welcomed us into the territory, softening the effect of what could be an intimidating structure.

"This looks a lot different than it used to," Jagger said as we entered what could only be described as a city center. An empty one, mind you, but on all sides there were small shops and businesses, selling every-thing from food to clothes. The doors of the estate were wide open, and the stairs were empty except for Aurora and an older man she was talking to.

"I know this is important, but we may not want to stay longer than we have to," Breaker said. "If we need to come back with more forces, fine, but I don't want Bexley in the crosshairs of a full-on rogue attack."

I frowned, not liking the idea of my mates being in the crosshairs of an attack either.

When the car came to a stop, I opened the door and slipped out, immediately offering a smile to Aurora. She didn't return it, her eyes darting down to the ground instead of holding my gaze.

"Welcome, Bexley Blackforge," the older man greeted, the use of my last name throwing me for a moment. It still sounded weird sometimes. "My name is Dyer."

"Nice to meet you," I replied, defaulting to politeness despite not knowing how this entire interaction was going to go.

The man responded with a calculating look at our group. "I would say it's nice to meet you as well, but things are rather tense with your arrival."

"Don't put that on her," Breaker rumbled, causing the man to pale.

"I understand this is a bit unexpected," I offered, "and maybe we should have called ahead..."

"Yes, yes, my daughter informed me why you're here." He sighed. "Very well, come in. That way everyone can stop hiding and go back to their commerce."

I hadn't noticed until then, but young and old

faces peeked around doors and shutters, listening in on our conversation. It probably also had to do with the fact that the sky was lightening now that my mates were more relaxed, the warm afternoon light filtering through the clouds to shine on the estate-turned-village.

"This must look different to you," Aurora said, finally holding my gaze.

"I don't completely remember what it looked like before," I admitted. Gage slipped his arm around me as we climbed the stairs, Breaker walking slightly ahead and Jagger behind, flanking me protectively.

Neither Aurora nor Dyer seemed to have much of an answer to that. We reached the top of the stairs and entered into a large hall, the ceilings nearly two stories tall and the walls covered in tapestries of gold, cream, and brown. Something about them jogged a small piece of my memory; a piece of my mind telling me that they were familiar, that we'd seen them before.

"Where do you need to go?" Dyer asked.

"I would try your family's old private quarters," Jagger suggested, causing my chest to relax. I literally had no idea what I would have said if he hadn't answered for me.

"That should work." I looked back at Dyer and Aurora. "Unless someone is in them?"

"We haven't touched those, actually," Dyer admitted. "We have respect for the dead, especially those who died under such tragic circumstances. The entire suite is preserved."

"Oh. Thank you," I said, not knowing how else to respond. But the gesture did touch me, and I suddenly had trouble finding my voice. "Did...did you know my parents?"

"No," Aurora said apologetically as she began leading us down a hall. "Some of the others did, though. They used to live under Flash Clan rule and chose to stay instead of being absorbed into the other clans' protection."

"Those original members of the clan requested we preserve the suite, and of course we agreed," Dyer explained. "The rest of the estate has been transformed into apartments and homes—especially the main floors."

"It's a good idea," I said, and Aurora's eyes widened in surprise that I'd agree. "Better than wasting resources on building a ton of houses—but what happened to the houses and villages that were on these lands originally?"

"Destroyed during the attack," Dyer said. "I wasn't here at the time—we traveled from the city—but it was bad enough that the survivors either fled or came here. No one stayed in the outer villages."

"This doesn't bother you?" Aurora asked, motioning to the doors we passed. Each was labeled with little address numbers, and mailboxes hung on the walls next to them. It was adorable.

"Why would it?" I asked seriously. "I get it, and it's been years."

"So sweet," Gage murmured, brushing his lips on top of my head.

Was I being sweet? It just felt rational to me.

"It has been. Our community isn't very large, and we only get a few new members each year, but we're strong," Dyer said. "This has become a safe haven for those who don't wish to live in the chaos of the city or under the heavy hand of the dragon clans."

"Heavy hand," Jagger mused.

Dyer offered him a cautious look. "I'm not saying it isn't needed to keep the peace, especially close to the city, but some of us want to live differently. In a community that's more integrated instead of all kinds of shifters being separated."

"We don't encourage separation," Breaker pointed out, "but we also don't tell people where to live and with whom."

"I'm not placing the blame all on your families," Dyer said as we began to climb a staircase. "I'm simply saying it's a reason people move here."

Surprisingly, my mates didn't seem upset. In fact, they seemed thoughtful, and I had to wonder if maybe this would change how they chose to lead their clan territories in the future. Maybe there was something to what Dyer was saying; maybe a more integrated system would be better. I knew for a fact in the Bronzeheart territory there were large strong villages, but all of them were separated by species of shifter—and if there weren't many others of your kind, you tended to live on the outskirts.

It had to be lonely. Isolating, even.

"Here we are."

My body froze as a very familiar door came into view. It was gold, embedded with black stones, and stood proudly within a stone wall. I let out a small exhale and walked forward, unsurprised when Breaker appeared next to me and opened up the heavy door, revealing...

Home.

It wasn't my home anymore, but tears instantly welled in my eyes. My hand came over my mouth to stifle the sad sound that threatened to leave me. The memories triggered by my moment with Breaker outside of the dorms, right before I marked him, had unlocked so much—had shown so much. But seeing it in person?

It seemed unreal.

Stepping into the massive room, my eyes went to the back wall where closed balcony doors and large windows featured a stunning view of Trabea. I walked slowly into the room and looked around at the many doors and halls leading off the main room, as well as the comfortable but aged furniture, colorful tapestries on the walls, and iron chandeliers that hung from the ceilings. Despite having been empty for the better part of a decade, there was a warmth and familiarity that stood out to me.

With tears in my eyes, I opened the balcony doors, the sight bringing forth so many memories from the back of my head. Breakfast with my parents at the stone table, playing games with my mates when they visited, and a million other things. I blinked away the tears as I let out a shaky breath at the overwhelming emotion that slammed into me like a tidal wave, rendering me nearly useless.

"Beautiful," Gage rumbled, appearing next to me. The early evening sunshine shone down on the southern mountains that I'd flown over as a child, making them sparkle like jewels. Lush greenery and tall trees covered every piece of land, from the estate through the valleys and up the mountains, and in the far distance, I could see the borders of the other clan territories. The Flash Clan really had overseen everything—the entire territory.

"Any memories sticking out?" Breaker asked, following us out onto the balcony. Jagger stayed inside, talking to Dyer.

I shook my head, knowing he meant specific memories about that night, and looked back around the space. "Could we go to my old bedroom?" My mom had woken me up from there...

"It's this way," Aurora said, pointing towards a hallway. I walked next to her down the hall she'd indicated, Breaker following behind at a distance. We went past several doors, and when she opened a light purple one embedded with gold stones, my heart stuttered.

It was like being stuck in a time warp.

The room was perfectly preserved, down to the soft pink and purple bedding and neatly folded blankets. I hesitated in the doorway, pain lancing through my chest. It was...too much. Too intense, and it wasn't evoking any memories regarding the incident —just pain.

Taking a controlled breath, I stepped into the room, still feeling nothing but sadness. I walked towards a child-sized table in the center of the room and found a stack of drawings, a small smile pulling on my lips. I picked up the top one, a depiction of three stick figures that I figured were supposed to be my parents and me, and underneath it was a similar drawing featuring four stick figures.

"This is a lot...and nothing about that night stands out to me," I told Breaker, not caring that Aurora was looking around curiously. She wasn't touching anything, so I could let it go. "But look what I found."

Breaker approached, his large frame almost funny next to the tiny table and chairs. When I handed him the picture, he chuckled.

"It's us," I said, moving my finger towards the birds in the sky. "And I bet these are our dragons."

"Keep these," Breaker said, a sentimental light in his gaze. "I love them."

I nodded and folded them in half before tucking them into his shirt pocket, pressing a kiss to his cheek when I went up on my toes.

"Sorry this isn't helpful," Aurora murmured, drawing my attention to where she stood looking over some books on the bedside table.

"It's okay." I took a deep breath, trying to shake myself. "It was good to see this. There's only one other place I can think to check—a woman named Rebecca's quarters. I think she was....a healer, maybe? She had a circular stone room—"

"With stained glass windows and herbs everywhere?" Aurora asked. I nodded and she offered a relieved smile, seemingly glad she could help—a far cry from our first encounter. "That was one of my favorite places to hang out when we first moved here. Follow me."

Her words should have filled me with hope, but the one thing that stood out? Rebecca wasn't there. Talking to her would have been the easiest way to get the answers we need.

I was just going to have to hope this room would do the trick. I didn't want this trip to be for nothing, especially after all of this.

I took a few more minutes to look around the family suite, but I was oddly relieved to leave. It sounded silly because I was glad I'd gone in there, glad I'd seen where I'd grown up, but the feelings it brought forth—the sadness—were overwhelming. As we walked along the same hallway we had taken here, I was surprised when Dyer opened a door that led to a separate, more private staircase.

We followed him and Aurora down, my mates on high alert. They didn't trust either of them, and I couldn't say whether I did or not. I didn't think they had any malicious intent towards us right now, but I also knew they wanted us out of here as soon as possible.

When we reached the bottom of the stairs, déjà vu hit me hard. I closed my eyes as memories of my mom walking me through this hall that night slammed into me and nearly left me breathless.

"Cupcake." Gage's voice was filled with worry.

"I'm okay," I promised, slowly opening my eyes and finding Aurora and Dyer staring at me in surprise. "This hallway is the one for sure."

Unable to help myself, I followed the phantom footsteps of my mom towards the door that featured front and center in my dream. I could practically hear my mom calling for Rebecca and pounding on the door, panic clear in her voice. When I reached the door, I didn't hesitate to turn the knob.

The hinges creaked loudly as the door swung open, and magic surged out to greet me.

Images flashed past me, ones of violence and blood. Ones that had my stomach churning. I could smell fire and hear cries of pain as a cloaked figure ran through smoke, darting to avoid darkly clothed men and women that filled the room, the ones enacting the chaos.

I couldn't look around, though, my focus riveted on the woman in the cape. I was tugged forward, soaring through the air after her as she fled the castle. I could practically feel her pain from here, and I knew before she even folded down the hood of her cloak that this was Rebecca.

Rebecca had run from the attack.

I didn't blame her, of course. But I was also surprised she'd escaped the soldiers busting into her room. I'd thought, even if I didn't want to admit it, that she'd died.

She hadn't, though, and as I followed her escape down an alley and through the forest, she eventually put down her hood to reveal her unique scaled appearance. She traveled for what felt like days on end, her sadness and anger turning to exhaustion. But she never stopped running for her life.

Finally, though, finally she reached the border to the territory next to us.

She crossed borders. That was how she'd survived. A portal appeared, a surge of magic of her own making filling the space in front of her as a word was whispered in my ear, faint but clear.

Sanguis.

• • •

My eyes flickered open, and I stared into the empty stone room before me. The magic that inhabited it had disappeared completely, as if its only purpose had been giving me that vision. As if it had been waiting for years just to show me where she'd gone.

Did Rebecca want me to find her?

"What just happened?" Aurora asked. "I've never felt magic like that in here; it came out of nowhere."

"It was waiting for her," Dyer explained.

"I know where Rebecca went and how she survived," I said softly.

"And she would know better than anyone what happened," Jagger murmured.

"When you moved in, was there anything in the estate that gave a clue as to who attacked? Does anyone remember?" I asked Dyer.

"Unfortunately not," he said, genuine sadness invading his features. "From what the survivors have told me, the attackers were unshifted and used brute human-like violence, and they wore dark unmarked clothes."

Rebecca, then. She would have the answers.

"Thank you for your help," I murmured, still feeling dazed as I looked to my mates. "We need to find Rebecca. She left this here for me, this spell to show that she escaped. We need to find her."

Breaker let out a low rumble. "And where did she go?"

I drew in my lip, Jagger's jaw tightening as he grunted, "I have a feeling I'm not going to like this."

"Sanguis."

Gage let out a legitimate growl. "The vampires. The fucking vampire territory."

Chapter 9

Jagger Silvershade

The Blackforge estate grew distant in our rearview mirror, Dyer and Aurora standing at the gates with the rest of the rogue land citizens gathered behind them. They'd been perfectly polite and helpful once we'd made it through the ambush, but they also hadn't made it a secret that they didn't like us being there. Their reaction left me torn because on one hand I understood it, but on the other hand I was pissed because they'd made Bexley uncomfortable. My hand rubbed her back in what I hoped was a soothing way as she turned into me, tearing her gaze away from the estate.

Tears pricked her eyes, and I could feel her pain through our bond, but not only pain—confusion, sorrow, loss, and oddly, relief as well. I knew it was from the heavy burden the memories placed on her and the stress of trying to discover what the hell had happened all those years ago.

"Breathe, little treasure," I murmured, running a finger along the side of her face.

"It's just a lot," she whispered, her voice catching. "Between the memories and them not wanting us there—which I really do understand—it's just...a lot."

"Why don't you try to rest until we get to the city?" I suggested. In addition to helping her, it would give the three of us a chance to talk. We were on the road that ran between the Bronzeheart and Silvershade territories towards the city, but it would be at least an hour or more until we got there. And before we did, we had to make a decision on a situation I wasn't fucking okay with in the least.

To travel into vampire territory. Sanguis.

The concept of the danger we'd be putting ourselves in had me pulling Bexley further into my side. She let out a small exhale as she melted against me, and I wasn't sure if she planned on following my suggestion until minutes later her eyes closed and her breathing evened out. Our girl had been through a lot in the past twenty-four hours. Hell, in the past two weeks.

"We can't go into fucking Sanguis," Gage finally

said. Breaker offered a sharp nod of agreement that I called bullshit on. If Bexley wanted to go, he would instantly flip sides and do what she wanted. I didn't blame him, of course, but I didn't see the point in denying the truth.

If Bexley wanted to go, we were going. I didn't have to like it though.

"Finding Rebecca is the only way to figure out what happened that night. I think Bex views it as her only way to help," I explained. Gage's expression darkened. In all of our opinions, Bexley didn't need to do anything—she was perfect as she was, discovering her memories as they filtered in. But I knew our girl, and I knew she wanted to *do* something to help. I also knew she wouldn't feel completely at peace until Linan Clanguard was proven to be the cause of her parents' deaths.

Honestly, she probably wouldn't feel peace until vengeance was taken. She would never admit that, but I could feel what her dragon wanted. I could feel the bloodlust raging beneath her animal's composure, waiting to break out at the right moment. Bexley was so fucking sweet, but the creature inside of her was lethal.

I'm not sure how she would feel about that once the realization eventually hit.

"Let's just get into the city," Gage finally said

after a prolonged moment. "We'll stay the night at one of the hotels in neutral territory. We should meet with some of them anyway, see what exactly Clanguard tried to convince them of."

"I don't want her around William's sleuth," Breaker said. "He's more of an asshole than I remember."

"He is," I agreed, "but we also don't want him as an enemy if we can help it. I think after Bexley's display of power, he won't be as quick to accuse her of lying."

"I think the water shifters, prey shifters, and avian shifters are where we should start," Breaker suggested after nodding in response to my analysis.

"The feline shifters didn't show," Gage suddenly realized.

He was right. Interesting.

"I have to assume that's a good thing... Maybe they don't talk to Clanguard?" I reasoned.

"We should see if they'll meet with us," Gage said.

"If the water, avian, prey, and feline shifters can see reason and understand we aren't coming for the city," Breaker said, "then the wolf shifters—hell, even the bear shifters—won't really matter."

"Let's arrange for a meeting right when we get there," I said, looking down at my watch. "It's already late, and I want to make sure Bex eats and gets some rest before we do anything tomorrow—especially if we're going to a different territory."

"I'll call," Breaker offered. "Let's have the meeting over dinner at the hotel. That way it's still neutral territory."

And the neutral territory was truly neutral. In fact, somehow it was one of the only things that all the leaders of Trabea could agree on—no one touched the neutral territory. It also allowed any travelers a place to stay without upsetting the balance of the city's hierarchy.

For example, if a shadow witch traveled here, they'd be safe. Or people like us who were planning to travel to the vampire territory.

I still couldn't get over that shit. It wasn't that I didn't believe we could protect her, but I had no interest in waging a war with the territory's leader if we ended up slaughtering a bunch of bloodsuckers. And if any of them tried to go for Bexley's blood, that is *exactly* what would happen.

"We should tell Dracula we're coming before we cross the border," I suggested. Gage offered a grunt of agreement, not willing to verbalize that this was a reality we had to deal with. It was a solid idea to let Dracula know, though—the immortal bastard was as lethal as you would expect, and I didn't want to disrupt the tenuous peace between our families and the vampire. The last thing we needed was a war between territories because they viewed our visit as some type of attack.

"We'll also let him know our mate is with us," Gage said, lowering his voice so as not to interrupt Breaker's quiet conversation on the phone, arranging for our meeting.

"So if anything happens he knows it's not a full-out war we're looking for," I chuckled, knowing exactly where his thoughts went.

I had always been protective over Bexley, even at a young age, but after reuniting after eight long years the urge to protect her could be overwhelming at times. Fates, it was always fucking overwhelming. My lips brushed the top of her head as I breathed in her delicate scent. Her scent that was still all over me.

I loved that shit.

The car fell into a quiet lull as early evening set on the territory and darkened the country landscape we passed through, Gage driving faster than normal. The concept of Bexley not having eaten all day was starting to weigh on us, Breaker's gaze moving back to her as he continued to make calls. Why the hell hadn't we fed her before we left?

"Good news. Alpha Spencer for the avian

shifters, Alpha Bowman for the water shifters, and Council Leader Annika for the prey shifters are willing to meet us for dinner in an hour," Breaker announced.

"The bad news," he drew out, "is that William isn't available—or at least that's what his admin staff is claiming—and the feline shifters didn't pick up. I left a message for the latter, but we'll see what happens."

"I don't want to fuck around with this," Gage said evenly. "We've made ourselves clear, and we've even given them a chance to align themselves with us outside of the meeting at DIA. If they don't come, then I consider them on the same level as Linan."

He was right. Hell, this was probably more than we should have done. With that being said, Bexley's safety was *everything,* and I was willing to have dinners with these other groups of shifters if it meant gaining allies— over half the city—to fight with us. After all, leadership wasn't only about pure force and power—it was about working with others, even when you didn't want to.

And I really didn't fucking want to.

As we neared the city, Bexley began to shift, letting out a small groan as she stretched her hands above her head and offered me a sleepy smile. Her eyes darted around the dark car before shooting up with interest, seeing the outline of the city approaching.

"Have you been?" I asked, running my fingers through her thick hair. I knew she had been when we were younger, but I had a feeling she didn't remember that.

"A few times." She cast me a wry smile. "Usually to go shopping. A lot of the imported products from Ordinarius went to the city first and then were brought out to us, but it was fun picking them right off the shelves sometimes."

"You brought her to the city." Breaker offered Gage an amused look because that sounded like the exact opposite of what our friend would choose to do.

"It was his mom," Bexley mused. "Gage shut the entire building down and wasn't happy about us going. Neither was his dad. But we still got our shopping done, which was fun. Plus, it was around the holidays, so we couldn't have it brought back to the estate because then everyone's presents wouldn't have been a surprise."

"You shut down an entire shopping center?" I barked out a laugh as Gage shrugged but kept driving. I mean, I didn't blame him, but that had to have pissed off the city shifters.

"He did." Bexley snuggled into me. "I'm excited to go with all three of you."

"Same, little treasure." I brushed my lips against her forehead. "We're going to get dinner before checking in, if that's okay with you."

"That would be amazing." She groaned. "I'm starving."

Gage sped up, and I nearly cracked a smile.

"You can eat while we talk," Breaker said, looking up from the phone. "We're meeting with some of the allied shifter groups so they can talk to us without Linan around."

Caution filled Bexley's gaze. "Okay... Are they mad about the fire explosion thing that I did?"

A smile broke onto my lips at the way her cheeks lit up. Only Bexley would be embarrassed at such an impressive show of power.

"No," Breaker said with surety. "And if they were, they could deal with it."

"Don't be ashamed of your power," I told her.

"If anything, they're probably scared, cupcake," Gage added.

Bexley's nose wrinkled in an adorable way that reminded me of a bunny. "Well, I don't love the idea of people being scared of me..."

Kissing the top of her head again, I decided to not respond because the fact of the matter was that they would be scared of her. Scared of her power. Scared of her mates. Scared of her family. Scared of her different way of thinking.

Bexley was scary in the most refreshing way possible.

When we finally reached the city, those concerns seemed to fly away—her interest on the view out the window, staring at the bright lights and large buildings. Our dark car didn't gather any attention until we reached the driveway of the luxury hotel we were staying at, the attendants immediately filing out and coming to open our doors.

I heaved a sigh. I knew it was protocol; I even understood why we were treated the way we were, but I also wanted to open the car door for my mate. I didn't need some other shifter doing it.

Getting out of the car, I offered the attendant a head nod before turning my back on him and holding the door open for Bexley. The smile she gave me was soft and sweet as her hand slid into mine, before wrapping her arms around my waist. I had to fight the urge to pick her up, instead leading her to the curb. The other two joined us with our bags in tow, not trusting them to the attendants. Something one of them was attempting to argue with Gage about.

Then Bexley's stomach rumbled.

"Ugh," she groaned, throwing her head back. "How freakin' embarrassing."

I couldn't help it anymore. I scooped her up and carried her into the luxury hotel, the lobby opulent with chandeliers, dark marble, and crystal. Bexley's attention was immediately riveted to all of it, and when we walked towards the entrance of the restaurant, I made a mental note to make sure she had a seat where she could still look at everything.

"Mr. Silvershade." The hostess at the front offered us a small smile before focusing completely on my mate, which had a visible effect on Bexley, her frame relaxing slightly. I didn't understand the interaction fully, but I suspected it had to do with Bexley's dragon.

Bexley wiggled down from my arms and followed behind the woman as I looked around the expensive restaurant, almost completely cleared of patrons. I appreciated that because it would be enough work keeping tabs on the people we were meeting with and ensuring they weren't threatening Bexley in any way—but an entire restaurant? That shit was distracting.

The hostess led us to a circular table that seated twelve, and I pulled out one of the leather chairs for Bexley, taking the seat to her left. Gage was to her right, with Breaker next to him. Our backs were to the wall, giving us all a view of the restaurant's entrance, which made me instantly feel more comfortable.

That was until two individuals approached the hostess.

"Who's that?" Bexley's brow furrowed, her gaze narrowed on one of the women with Alpha Fangce walking towards us.

"The feline shifters," Breaker said with a long sigh. "Alpha Fangce and his sister. I can't remember her name though."

Bexley nodded, her posture straightening as the woman met her gaze and offered a dark smile. My hand slid onto Bex's leg as I let out a low rumble.

I had a feeling this meeting wasn't going to be nearly as peaceful as we had assumed.

Chapter 10

Bexley Blackforge

Normally I didn't like to make assumptions about how people would act before meeting them...but I wasn't extending the same grace to the woman walking towards us, mainly because her eyes had been glued to my mates from the moment she stepped into the restaurant. I kept my lips pressed together, holding in a defensive sound as her eyes moved over Breaker, to Gage, and then Jagger...before finally resting on me.

I wasn't sure what I'd expected her to do after noticing them—maybe the same as the hostess? She'd noticed my mates as well, but when she saw I was with them, she stopped looking at them. It was something I'd noticed was common with shifters even on campus, like being someone's mate transcended even dominance stuff.

This woman did not do the same, nor did she seem to care. In fact, her smile grew, and she shot me a wink before returning her attention to my mates.

A wave of possessiveness rolled over me. I wanted to stand up to shield my mates from this... this...I didn't know what to call her. I didn't give a crap who she was; I wanted her away from my men. If she was going to be at this meeting, I wasn't sure anything would get done without conflict.

"You should've let us know you were coming," Breaker said, standing and meeting the hand of Alpha Fangce.

"Treya and I were already out," he explained. His blue eyes flickered over Gage and Jagger and he greeted them with a hard nod, but he completely avoided looking at me. "We didn't want any misunderstandings, so we just came right over."

"Yes, misunderstandings always seem to be an issue with shifters," Treya purred—*literally freakin' purred*—as her gaze moved from her brother back to me.

I had to admit, she was objectively stunning, her looks enhanced by the feline way she prowled around the table. Her white-silver hair was pulled back in an intricate braid, and she wore a simple yet expensive looking pair of tailored pants and shirt. Unfortunately, she was also wearing heels that clicked as she made her way towards us, her intention all too clear.

Nope. No way.

One minute I was seated between my mates and the next I was standing directly in her path, blocking her from sitting next to Jagger. Her smile only grew as a dangerous sound left my throat.

"Bexley, right?" Treya's eyes flashed with amusement. "I heard we had a new dragon running around —I didn't realize it was a lost heir, though. How cute."

I didn't know how to respond because everything I wanted to say verged on the line of being a total jerk.

"What's even cuter, though, are your mates—"

"Call your sister off," Gage said above my growl before she could finish her sentence.

Fangce heaved a sigh. "It's not what you or your mate think. She doesn't normally act like this."

I felt my brows rise in confusion, the scowl Treya shot her brother only adding to the mess. For just a moment, her confidence completely disappeared and she looked far younger... Until she looked back at me as if the interaction hadn't happened.

"What do you mean?" I asked, Treya rolling her eyes as if his words didn't bother her.

"Don't listen to him; I know exactly what I'm doing—"

"She does this shit all the time. She's just testing dominance because she recently figured out that she's an alpha," Fangce explained, his gaze on his little sister in understanding. "She just turned eighteen."

Oh.

Treya let out a low growl of frustration before deflating and walking back around the table. I was left a bit stunned as I kept my gaze on her, not completely trusting this turn of events.

"I'm confused," I admitted.

"Don't be." Treya waved her hand in the air as if she could erase the past few minutes. "I just haven't met another female alpha my age, and I wanted to—well, I don't even know, but he ruined it."

"You wanted to mess with me about my mates and try to assert yourself as more dominant?" It was weird that she would actively want to do that, but the way she nodded enthusiastically had me feeling a bit bad for her. Why would she want that, let alone seek to cause a problem with a woman she didn't even know?

"Treya has been very sheltered—she wasn't allowed to be a shifter, at least to the extent most of us are—until our parents passed," Fangce explained.

Treya shot him a scowl, but beneath the facade, I could see immense sadness and disappointment. I'd been sheltered by the Bronzehearts, but I'd never been told to not embrace my nature...

I just hadn't known my nature.

Still. Even if I didn't like how she'd been treated, it didn't excuse her behavior.

"Don't mess with my mates," I warned her, almost surprised by the dominance that seeped through my words. One that had her sinking back. "If you want to work on shifter stuff or train together, we could try that. I haven't had a chance to yet—"

"Yes." Her eyes lit up with excitement as she repeated herself. "Yes."

"Okay." I slowly sat down back between my mates and rested my hand in Gage's. "Works for me."

Sort of.

Treya relaxed a bit at that and started playing on her phone, and Fangce just shrugged, looking exhausted.

I had no idea where to go from here. This was a weird situation, but I was glad the animosity between his sister and me had dissipated. I had never reacted so extremely to the simple intention I could feel coming off someone.

"You said you wanted to come so there were no

misunderstandings?" Gage asked, returning the conversation to our original track.

"Yes. We never met with Clanguard, but Annika told us what happened at DIA," Fangce explained. "We didn't know the best way to assure you of our alliance, so we showed up here."

"We appreciate the effort," Jagger said. "Hopefully, we won't need any of this—hopefully it can be resolved when Linan realizes he has no support."

"The problem with Linan—" The familiar voice had me looking over to see Alpha Spencer walking with her mate, Kelvin, towards the table, her elegant frame covered in green silk. "—is that his pack is the size of all of ours combined."

"Spencer, good to see you," Fangce said as Kelvin took a seat next to him.

"I'm surprised to see you," Spencer drew out as she sat on the other side of her mate, Kelvin acting as a barrier between her and Fangce. "And your little sister as well."

Treya's eyes darted up from her phone, and she offered a small, awkward smile to the woman before looking back down.

I didn't understand her at all—she'd been brimming with confidence and aggression, and now she seemed like a different woman altogether.

"I didn't want any misunderstandings," Fangce repeated.

"Yes, well Linan, I'm sure, will take it personally —piece of shit," she growled, making my eyes widen. Her gaze finally moved to mine as she smiled, mirth playing at the edges of her expression that hadn't been there when we first met.

"And you, Bexley Blackforge, bother him a lot," she continued. "Especially with that little fire stunt."

"He was talking about my parents," I said meekly, hoping that explained it. Her answering expression told me it did.

"Alpha Bowman," Gage greeted, eyes moving in the direction of the hostess stand. A small woman was tucked into the aquatic shifter's side, and I blinked in surprise because there was no real way to describe her besides *unique*.

First off, her hair was a rainbow of blues, purples, and greens, and her skin seemed to sparkle like scales. Her eyes were massive, almost purple, as she looked around the restaurant with curiosity, leaning further into Alpha Bowman as they drew nearer to the table. When they reached us, I was so caught up in watching her unsure yet curious mannerisms that I didn't realize everyone was introducing themselves.

"Angel," Alpha Bowman said to the woman,

"this is Bexley Blackforge, mate to the three other heirs."

"It's wonderful to meet you," she offered, her voice almost nonexistent in pitch but perfectly clear.

"Same," I said with a friendly smile as they took their seats, revealing possibly the biggest surprise of the night.

Annika and William.

The entire table, which had been talking in relaxed conversational tones before, tensed at the sight of William. At least that was how my mates and I reacted.

"William." Breaker stood. "What are you doing here?"

"I invited him," Annika said boldly—a manner opposite of what you'd expect from a prey shifter, even if she was their leader. In fact, her confidence seemed unbreakable—far more intense than she'd been at DIA.

"I wanted to make my intention clearer than I did at the meeting," William explained, taking the final seat next to Annika. "I question out of the protectiveness I have over my sleuth and nothing more. I have no allegiance to Linan, but I understand that's how it came across."

My brows went up as Gage let out a defensive

sound at the name 'Linan' before saying, "He seemed to think you were on the same page as him."

"He did," William said, "which is exactly how I want it to stay—at least until I can find out what he's planning."

"Planning?" I swallowed, feeling a surge of nervousness.

"I think we can all agree that he has *something* planned," Alpha Spencer said evenly. "The question is—what is it? And what do we do about it?"

The 'we' stood out to me, and as the waiter approached, passing out menus, I felt a small flame of hope in my chest. One that told me that maybe— just maybe—we would have more help figuring out what Clanguard was up to than we ever expected.

I couldn't remember the last time I'd had a meal that was so long and filled with so many courses. Don't get me wrong, I wasn't complaining, but by the fourth course I found myself wanting to curl up and go to bed. A nap was one thing, but a good night's sleep was what I really needed to feel better. I prob- ably could have fallen asleep at the table if I hadn't been so interested in the conversation.

While the group didn't know what Clanguard

was planning specifically, everyone promised to keep us well informed under the guise of continuing to be in 'talks' with him about the situation. As the night wore on, the true distaste the other shifters had for Linan Clanguard and his pack became clear.

The pack was apparently committing crimes throughout the city—fraud, theft, even murder—a fact that was so well known that people didn't even question it anymore. Unfortunately, while everyone knew he was responsible, there was no evidence to directly pin him. Everything was blamed on one of his pack members...of which he had many.

His wolf pack made up more than fifty percent of the city, and the remaining five groups of shifters made up the rest. That number was concerning on its own; even more so if he was trying to amass more allies.

"Bexley," Alpha Bowman's mate, whose name I learned was Angelica, said. She'd taken the seat next to Jagger but spent a lot of the time on Bowman's lap. I would have been bothered by her sitting by my mate, but it was unavoidable—someone had to. At least the person who'd sat next to him was obviously obsessed with her own mate. In fact, this may have been one of the only times she had looked away from him.

"What's up?" I asked, leaning forward on the

table so I could hear her. Gage's hand was on my leg, and Jagger's ran up my back in a comforting move.

"I just didn't realize that you would be here. It's really nice to meet you," she said, her personality upbeat despite her shyness. "My family was really close to the Blackforge family before your parents passed—we probably met as kids."

"Really? That's really cool." I couldn't help the smile that grew on my lips. "Did you come to the estate a lot?"

"Yes, although the friendship was considered a bit odd, considering." She motioned to herself, and I arched a brow in confusion.

"Her family are angelfish shifters," Jagger explained.

"Ah." I nodded and looked back at her. "Fish and dragons being friends? Sounds reasonable to me."

"That's what I thought." She smiled softly. "When you come into the city next, you'll have to come by our place. It's not as large as the dragon territories, but it's pretty fun."

"I would love that," I told her. I really would. Between the rogue lands, the city, and now Sanguis... I was excited about all of the new experiences that'd opened themselves to me. Sure, it wasn't for the best reason in the world, and what we were trying to figure out was somewhat sad....but I was traveling with my mates.

I couldn't regret that.

When Breaker and Gage suddenly stood a minute later, followed by Jagger and the others, I realized the meeting was over. Everyone was saying their goodbyes, and even though I was happy with how the meeting had gone, I couldn't help but look forward to getting into bed. I could feel the same sense of contentment in my mating bond, and I let Gage pick me up the minute we were near the elevators, happy to be able to fully relax.

Plus, now that we were alone, I didn't feel the pressing need to show that I was a 'strong' shifter. It was something I liked to fight against anyway—I didn't think it was necessary to always be showing your strength—but when there were so many high-level shifters around, my dragon naturally pulled it out in me.

My eyes grew heavy, the classical elevator music and the strong, steady heartbeat of my mate lulling me to sleep before we even reached our room.

Chapter 11

Bexley Blackforge

The steam from the shower wrapped around me, creating a perfect cocoon of peace to wake up to—well, until one of my mates freakin' opened the bathroom door.

A low, pained groan filled the space, and I opened one eye to see Gage offering me a heated look from the door, his eyes roaming down my frame before he grumbled and walked out. I let out a small giggle, unable to help myself, because it wasn't my fault he chose to open the door. What did he think, that I would be showering with clothes on?

I did wonder why he was coming in here, though, especially if it wasn't for any fun reason. Moments later I got my answer after I turned off the shower and wrapped myself in a towel, feeling fully cleansed after everything that had happened yesterday.

More importantly, I felt ready for everything we would have to face in Sanguis.

"*Mo chuisle.*" Breaker was leaning against the bathroom doorway, subtle but very clear desire flickering in his unique eyes as he looked over my towel. "We're planning to leave soon, but if you need more time we can arrange for the driver to come back later."

"No, I'm going to be ready pretty fast." I motioned to my pile of clothes and cosmetic bag. "Just needed to shower after sleeping for so long."

"I'm glad you got some rest," he said solemnly as he stepped towards me, his thumbs brushing the underneath of my jaw and tilting it upward. "I worry about you overdoing it. Especially since all this memory shit Rebecca set up seems to trigger your magic."

"It does." I sighed. "But it's worth it. Plus, I want to learn how to use my magic, and we don't exactly have a lot of time to train between everything else going on."

Breaker's gaze flashed with concern. "Say the word and we can forget about this shit with Clanguard. He's a problem, but we can let our parents handle it and go back to school."

I smiled at his attempt to make me feel better, but I knew the truth. "You guys wouldn't stop, not really. If there's a threat, you're going to monitor it. The only thing that would change is that I'd be out of the loop."

Breaker grunted and nodded, knowing I was right, as he pulled me against him and dipped his head. When his lips brushed mine I let out a pleased sound, nearly scowling when he pulled away once again and stepped back towards the door.

"We're waiting in the main room; take your time," he said before disappearing.

I didn't take my time, though, because there was a nervous yet excited energy under my skin at the idea of going to a new territory. I had traveled a little bit but not much, staying insulated in the Bronze-heart estate for most of what I'd been able to remember until now, and had never really questioned it. Now, though? Now I was keen to see what else was out there.

After quickly styling my hair into two long braids and applying some light makeup, I slipped into what I deemed to be the best 'adventure' outfit ever.

The pants were high-waisted khaki cargo with gold flecks on the normally boring material. The pockets were lined in small gold studs that matched the belt I paired with it, and my small pink half top perfectly matched the combat boots I'd chosen.

Giving myself a once-over in the mirror, I added a matching khaki jacket and grabbed my stuff before leaving the bathroom.

"Holy shit." Jagger froze, his eyes running over me, and I nearly ran into him.

"Isn't it cute?!" I exclaimed, walking over to the bed and adding my old clothes and cosmetic bag into my luggage. I let out a surprised sound as Jagger appeared behind me, one hand gripping my hip and the other tilting my chin up, his eyes deepening to charcoal.

"Cute," he growled, "is not the word I would use to describe how you look, little treasure."

"What word would you use?" I whimpered as I felt just how hard he was against me—how much my outfit affected him.

"Dangerous," Gage said as he stepped into the doorway. His words had a blush invading my cheeks. "Dangerous, cupcake, because any fucking man who looks at you in that is going to want what's ours."

My toes curled as I swallowed, feeling a rush of adrenaline and excitement. I hadn't expected their reaction to this outfit, but I was absolutely in love with it.

"Well..." I teased, turning out of Jagger's arms. "I'm not changing, so I guess I'm dangerous."

Breaker chuckled from the other room, clearly listening in. As I walked past Gage, I tried to put a bit more sway into my hips than usual, his chest producing a low sound that had me shivering. Jagger said something to him that had him grunting in agreement as I escaped the room and went towards Breaker. While I enjoyed their reaction, I had a feeling that they would try to cover me up or make me change.

That wasn't happening. I loved this outfit!

"I love it too," Breaker said, pulling me against him before brushing his lips against mine once again. "But if you want it intact and wearable, we should probably leave."

"Because they would ruin it?" I scowled, looking back at Jagger and Gage, who looked like they were conspiring to do just that.

"Yes, but probably not how you're imagining." Breaker chuckled, and I arched a brow but let him lead me from the room.

"*You* don't want to ruin it?" I asked softly, feeling momentarily insecure.

Breaker's gaze snapped down to me, and a surprised noise left my throat as he backed me up against the wall in the blink of an eye, his usually calm facade falling away. His fingers tangled in my hair, his grip firm as he kissed me hard and deep. I could feel his need for me surging through our bond and into my very veins, and when he pulled away, I felt breathless at the intensity in his gaze.

"I want to fucking *ruin* you, Bexley. Don't ever think differently."

Holy fates. I felt dazed as he flashed me a dangerous smile and then pulled me into his side, leading me forward as if he hadn't just...well, whatever the heck he'd just done! Also, the idea of Breaker wanting to ruin me sounded amazing.

"Are you two good?" Jagger asked as we slipped into the elevator. I looked up at him, trying to look like Breaker hadn't just kissed the shit out of me.

"Just assuring her of something," Breaker said. I blinked and looked down at my pink combat boots, my cheeks flushing.

"Must have really been *something* if she's blushing." Jagger chuckled.

"Doesn't take a lot," Gage teased. I shot him a scowl, though I was unable to stay mad at him because of the soft affection in his gaze.

"I don't even blush that much!" I countered, all of them flashing smiles that said that I probably blushed even *more* than I even realized.

"Of course," Breaker agreed, his eyes twinkling with humor.

When the elevator doors opened, I huffed,

pretending to be upset as I walked ahead. I let out a small surprised squeak as Gage scooped me up and carried me towards the door. I could tell people were watching us in surprise, but I kept my focus on my mate, who was staring down at me with so much warmth and love that I couldn't help but melt.

I knew my mates were nervous about our trip to Sanguis, or at least concerned at what we might face, but they were managing to keep the tone light, probably for my benefit. I didn't realize it until recently, but with our bond, I was extremely reactive to their emotions, and I loved that they were trying, even with this, to protect me.

Although I wanted to be strong for them as well.

"How far is the portal?" I asked as the four of us got into the back of a dark SUV. There was a partition up between the driver and us so I didn't know who was in the front seat, but with how relaxed my mates were, I had to assume it was someone they were comfortable with.

"Five minutes at most," Jagger said. "We'll have to use our magic to open it, but it'll be pretty easy from there."

I nodded and watched the city skyscape pass by, shifters going about their day and paying no mind to the dark SUV amongst the other traffic. I had to admit, part of me wondered what it would be like to live in a large urban center like this. What if the Bronzehearts hadn't found me? What if I'd been raised on the streets? How different would my story have been?

"Here we are," Breaker announced as the car came to a stop. Gage got out to talk to the driver as Breaker and Jagger stepped out with me to the other side. I was confused at first where we were, a large seemingly abandoned building in front of us, but the minute I let my dragon out even a little bit—feeling the area around me—I was drawn towards the building.

I walked towards the heavy wooden door, Gage and Jagger following behind me as Breaker jogged ahead and opened it for us. I offered him a small smile and squeezed his hand in passing as I stepped into the building, my eyes immediately focusing on the large arch in the middle of the empty warehouse.

Much like the one that led into DIA, this was crafted of hand-carved wood, but it looked far more weathered and aged. I couldn't help but run my fingers along it as the energy that vibrated through it seemed to roll over my skin. I had never opened a portal before—I knew the one for DIA could only be opened by the headmistress—but this one...

My dragon surged forward, something I would normally try to stop because the feeling was so unfamiliar, but this time I didn't.

Instead I let her come to the surface while still maintaining my human form.

I couldn't describe what happened next except through sensation. The scent of ozone filled the air. Thunder boomed and vibrated my eardrums. The hair on my arms stood up as electricity cracked beneath my fingers on the portal arch. Lightning filled the room in dangerous flashes. All at once, it was like an explosion of power pulsated out of me and into...

The portal.

I stumbled back as the mercurial liquid center came alive, like glassy water. I felt Jagger's firm chest behind me as he let out a curse, keeping me pulled against him.

"Did she just—"

"Open a portal on her own?"

"Yeah, she fucking did," Breaker muttered.

Holy fates.

I knew the Bronzehearts had claimed I would be strong, but until this moment I hadn't fully understood what they meant. Now as I stared at the open portal, surrounded by my three mates, a nervous energy filled me.

"I'm guessing that's not normal?" I said, my voice small.

"It usually takes two, sometimes three storm dragons to open the portal," Jagger said, awe tinting his voice. "I think each of us have been able to open it on our own maybe once or twice, but it wasn't easy—pulling on all the magic it requires can leave us feeling drained. "

"I feel good," I said softly. "Really good."

"Crazy," Breaker mumbled, "but amazing."

"Good job, cupcake," Gage said, pressing a soft kiss to the top of my head. "Let us know if you start to feel bad—we can handle the transport element from here."

I nodded and curled against Jagger as we walked forward, the four of us entering the portal at the same time, darkness closing over us.

Unlike the portal into DIA, this felt like it stretched on. I could feel my mates around me, and flashes of light filled the air like a stormy sky, but I couldn't see anything. It made no sense, but the effect eventually had me closing my eyes because of how my stomach twisted and turned. The cool wind brushing over me felt good against my burning skin, my dragon trying to push out in response to such an intense draw of magic.

Then, all at once, it was over.

I groaned as I stumbled forward. Jagger caught me up against him, an icy wind hitting us almost immediately and causing a shiver to roll over my frame. I curled into my mate as wet rain hit our skin, causing him to curse up a storm.

"This way!" Gage called out, and while I couldn't see anything, Jagger led us forward. I wanted to look around, but the howling wind was so intense that I didn't risk it. At least until we were more shielded from the elements.

"Are you okay, little treasure?" Jagger asked. I nodded and looked around as I gathered myself, seeing a flash of the portal in the distance before it closed, settling between some trees. The four of us were now sheltered on a stone pathway protected by tall, broad pines.

I peeked out and immediately my brows went up, noticing a large town in the distance. It wasn't far, maybe a few miles at most, the dark gothic architecture of the homes standing out against the cloudy sky. When the wind settled suddenly, my mates were already talking.

"Wait." I turned sharply towards them. "Was that wind because of us?"

"Yeah." Breaker ran a hand through his hair. "When we travel through portals, it usually causes a disturbance. That's why us three heirs usually travel separately onto campus."

Interesting.

When we retreated from the shelter of the pines, I was able to see that the path ran north to south, with the neighborhood to the south. Trees blocked my view to the north, but the terrain sloped slightly upwards.

"So what now? Which way?" I asked curiously.

"South," Jagger said. "At least that's my best guess. We portalled into the southern portion of Sanguis, right by one of the original cities, which has been long abandoned."

"So why would we go there?"

"Sanguis is set up so that the leader of the territory, Dracula, is in the northern mountains, and the larger more modern city is in the central part of the territory. Those areas are the most inhabited, and Rebecca, if she stayed here, would have avoided both Dracula and the city if she were trying to hide. So if we eliminate those two..."

"It would leave that." Gage nodded towards the town in question. It made sense. While it didn't look abandoned from here, I did have to admit that the noise that usually accompanied people going about their daily lives was lacking.

"If we head that way, maybe my dragon will pick up on something," I said hopefully. I had no idea how it worked, this trail of memory crumbles Rebecca had me following, but it was the best suggestion I had at the moment.

Settled on our plan, the four of us began walking, the cold gray skies beautiful in an eerie way. I tucked my jacket further around me, and when Breaker came up next to me, I leaned into his side. I hadn't known what to expect from this territory, but so far it had been rather quiet.

And, unfortunately, devoid of vampires.

Or maybe that was a good thing...I didn't think so, though. If Alina was awesome, it only made sense that there'd be others like her, equally as cool. Although hadn't she said something about them not being good? I would trust her opinion on that and reserve my judgment, then.

I hoped my friend was okay. We weren't super close, but with everything going on at the school it made me nervous not knowing how she was doing or what was going on in her sector.

"Wow," I murmured as we stopped at a stone archway with an impressive gargoyle on top, a menacing look marring its face as it stared down at us. On the other side, the stone road turned to a paved street lined by large mansions and estates that only grew in size as it went further along. I could tell my mates were listening for movement, and my eyes darted around curiosity, wondering if we'd be able to hear vampires if they didn't want to be detected.

I mean, Alina had been so freakin' quiet that it still blew my mind.

"Keep guarded," Gage warned, taking the lead. Jagger walked behind us, positioning me right in the center of all my mates. It had my dragon listening ten times harder because we didn't like the idea of my mates being taken off guard.

It was around four blocks in that I began to feel as if we were being watched. I came to a stop, my eyes scouting the tops of the buildings as a defensive rumble left my lips.

"Cupcake?" Gage asked.

"Someone is watching us," I murmured.

"We should ignore them. It's not worth the bull-shit," Breaker suggested. I didn't disagree, but I also doubted we were going to have a choice in the matter.

Moments later, I was proven right as a dark chuckle filled the empty city blocks.

We paused in our pursuit forward, my mates not looking worried, exactly, but a defensive protective edge filled the air. I kept my head on a swivel, so I didn't miss the moment when a dark shadow stepped out of a nearby doorway, followed by other figures emerging from shadows along the street.

There were a lot of them, and they'd been watching us for some time.

The only question—what did they want?

Chapter 12

Bexley Blackforge

My gaze immediately focused on the first vampire I'd noticed—the one that had chuckled and somehow signaled to the others that it was time to make themselves known. I wasn't positive what I expected him to look like but...it wasn't this. Maybe It was bad of me to judge because this obviously wasn't the best place to live, but compared to the few other vampires I'd seen, and of course Alina...this guy looked rough.

In fact—my gaze darted around at the gathered group—they *all* looked really rough.

"What do we have here? Shifters?" the man asked, stalking towards us.

"Shifters with a lot of magic," a woman added.

"This isn't a good idea," Gage warned, his voice

laced with threatening intensity as his power expanded out around us. "We aren't here to cause a problem—we're searching for something."

"For someone," I added. "Her name is Rebecca."

No one seemed to care. The man shrugged. "Never fucking heard of her. But it doesn't matter, because your journey ends here."

"Fucking shit," Jagger muttered, directing his next comment to Breaker. "If they attack, you need to remove her immediately."

Breaker's gaze darkened as he looked around. "I will. My dragon won't allow anything else—he's fucking furious."

"You don't want to do this," Gage warned again.

"We *have* to do this," someone growled. "We need to feed."

"And her blood smells amazing," another woman added. I couldn't contain the way I cringed at the hunger painted across her expression.

Above, thunder cracked as Breaker let out a noise that had half of the crowd shrinking back. Jagger rolled his shoulders back, not looking concerned as much as annoyed with the vampires. Their confidence never ceased to amaze me, and when Gage pressed a light kiss to my forehead, I nearly melted.

"Get her out of here."

His words must have sealed the deal because the

minute Breaker had me in his arms, an enraged, impatient cry left one of the vampires as they surged forward. I cursed and clung onto him as he raced away, only setting me down once we were tucked away inside an abandoned mansion near the neighborhood's entrance, the distant sound of violence only that—distant.

"Breaker," I hissed, looking out the window of a room on the second floor. "We shouldn't have just left them—"

"They're fine," he said roughly. "If they wanted to, they could slaughter triple that amount. Right now they'll try to defuse the situation, but if you were in the crossfire they'd react more violently."

"Because of your dragons?" I asked softly, turning to look back at him. "Because of the threat they pose—

"Breaker," I gasped. A tremble went over my skin, my wrists pinned above me, as Breaker took deep breaths, trying to calm himself down. I was surprised by his intensity, though maybe I shouldn't have been—hadn't he told me this was what was laying under the surface?

His attempt at composing himself was a failed effort, though, and I wasn't making it any better because I could feel how hard he was, causing my own need to saturate the space. He was so much taller than me, his height making it so that his cock was pressed right against my stomach, its massive size obvious despite the clothing between us. I couldn't help but run my tongue over my lips, imagining what it would be like to have him in my mouth.

"I just need a minute—just a minute."

He needed more than a minute, and I could tell just how worked up he was by the way a slight tremble ran over him, his control faltering. I wanted to make him feel better, but I was stuck, pinned to the wall and absolutely at his mercy.

"Let me help you," I whispered, tilting my chin up and my eyes running over his lips. "I can help you calm down."

Breaker's laugh was rough and filled with a darkness that I loved far too much. "The only way you could help me calm down is if you spread those pretty thighs for me, *mo chuisle*, and let me come inside of you. Let me mark you."

Holy fates.

I whimpered, pressing my thighs together as I grew more wet, imagining the picture he was painting.

"But we can't do that here—not when they're out there listening to every fucking sound you make, wanting your blood for themselves," he growled, the feral noise vibrating through his chest and across my skin. His skin shimmered as scales seemed to appear and disappear underneath it, barely showing but enough to know the thought of the vampires getting my blood had him losing it.

"What if you could still mark me but we don't go all the way?" I asked. "That way they won't hear it—"

Breaker groaned, one hand coming down from where it had been pinning my wrists and sliding down to my waist, gripping me in a tight hold. My skin broke out into shivers, and my nipples hardened against the lace material of my bra, showing through the half top. Breaker's gaze was filled with indecision, and I knew I needed to convince him.

Breaker was always going to protect me, but this was something we both wanted—even if there were vampires around.

"I need you, even if it's just a little bit," I explained breathlessly.

"Fuck, I can't say no to you," he growled, dropping my hands and going down on one knee I moaned softly as he trailed soft kisses down my stomach while he unbuckled my pants and tugged them down.. The feral noise he let loose told me he could see how wet I was, my panties soaked.

"Turn and place your hands on the window," he said softly, his voice throaty and dangerous. I did so immediately, arching my back, Breaker gripping my ass and squeezing it roughly. I wanted so badly to feel his rough fingers against my wet heat, and I spread my legs as far as I could with my pants still around my ankles, urging him on.

"Fates, you are so wet. I can tell how much you want this." His voice was filled with need. "I'm going to give you relief and mark you, but we can't fully fuck. Not with all these bastards around. They don't deserve to hear you."

"Just a little bit," I promised breathlessly, though I wasn't sure I could keep it. I gasped, pure excitement and need rolling through me when his fingers pushed away my lace thong and slid along my wet slit, Breaker rolling his thumb over my clit before sinking a finger inside of me. I gripped the window sill as his other hand sank into my hair, keeping a firm hold on me.

"I'm not sure I'll be able to resist if I put my cock anywhere near your pussy," he growled, frustrated with himself more than anything.

"Please, Breaker," I whimpered, not even caring that I was begging. I nearly moaned in anticipation when I heard his pants unzip, his hand moving from my wet center to his cock. I jolted, moaning his name as his hard cock pressed right against my slit.

"Holy fuck," he hissed, pressing his forehead

down against my back while barely pressing into me. "I don't have this type of control."

"I want you to mark me," I said, not used to the demand in my voice but also feeling a sense of victory as his dragon responded, the dominant noise that left him completely primal. I whimpered as he pushed forward just enough that he began to stretch me. My pussy tightened, wanting to grip around him, as I let out a sound of frustration at him not being further inside.

"I could come inside you right now." Breaker cursed. "Seeing your tight pussy wrapped around my tip like this has me wanting to bury myself so fucking deep inside of you."

"Do it." I pushed back, urging him on, and he groaned as another inch of his cock sank inside of me. A delicious shiver rolled over me, and I swear I felt warmth flood me, only making me that much more wet. I loved the need Breaker had for me, and when his grip fell from my hair onto my waist, trying to get a better hold on me, I knew he was close to breaking.

"I can't." His voice was sharp and hard. "Damnit, Bexley."

"Breaker." I looked back at him, my need for him obvious in my voice. "I don't care if they hear us. I want them to hear how good you make me feel."

Breaker's gaze was completely black, and I saw the snap happen. All at once his grip turned harder on me and he surged forward, filling me completely.

"Breaker!" I felt dizzy with satisfaction, a twinge of pain accompanying the sensation of being stretched by him, as pleasure blossomed in my abdomen. My clit pulsed, and I squeezed around him as my knees nearly gave out.

His lips ran over the back of my neck as he let out a dangerous noise. "You feel so fucking perfect, *mo chuisle*. I could live inside of this pussy and it still wouldn't be enough. I would still crave you every single second—"

I whimpered as he pulled out and slammed back in, my eyes rolling back as his hand slid over my hip and began to strum my clit while pounding in and out of me.

There was such a primal intensity when it came to Breaker; I could feel his creature right under the surface. Mine as well. They were mating in the purest sense, and I could barely see straight as his hard and wide length continued to pummel in and out of me. His dangerous vibrating voice was against my ear, telling me how good I was at taking him.

How amazing it felt to be inside of me.

I could feel my orgasm building, and I knew without a doubt it was going to absolutely detonate me. I moaned loud enough that his hand came over my mouth, and a possessive, rough tone filled his voice. "I don't want them hearing the perfect fucking noises you make."

I ran my tongue over his skin, and I didn't even bother fighting the urge to bite down—hard.

He groaned my name as his own teeth skimmed my throat, not biting down but teasing me. I wanted more. I wanted to feel him rutting into me as he marked the back of my neck, biting down and holding himself there. Thunder and lightning cracked outside, turning everything electric as his power electrified my very soul.

"Breaker!" I cried out his name as he slammed into me one last time before burying his teeth in the back of my neck. The wind whipped around us, and the howling made my ears ring as my climax crashed over me. My knees gave out as I held on to the windowsill, and I felt our bond solidify itself, the threads coated in pure gold.

Melted euphoric pleasure rolled over every inch of my body as I floated in the heaven of Breaker being buried inside of me, both his length and his teeth. His hold on me was primal, and I couldn't move even if I wanted to. He was completely dominating me in every single way, and it allowed me to relax in a way I didn't think was possible.

"Bexley," Breaker groaned, releasing my neck before gripping my throat and tilting my head back to kiss me hard. When he pulled away, I saw blood, probably from us biting each other, both having broken skin. The metallic scent of it and storms surrounded us as I held his intense gaze.

"That was—" I whimpered as he pulled out just slightly, before pushing back in.

"So fucking amazing," he growled before finally pulling out. "Stay still for me."

He pulled my panties up and cupped me with his hand, keeping our cum right between my thighs as he grazed his lips over my new mating mark. When he fixed my pants and then his as well, I almost sank to my knees, feeling absolutely exhausted and exhilarated at the same time.

Luckily, he promptly picked me up and kissed me hard on the lips.

"I think they all probably heard us," I said lightly as Breaker let out a deep, possessive rumble.

They had totally heard us—there was zero doubt about that.

"I love and hate that," he admitted. "I want them to know just how good you're being fucked, but I don't want them to imagine that—fucking ever."

"I think everyone in the damn territory knows." Gage's familiar voice had me smiling as Breaker walked us down a set of stairs in the abandoned home, Gage and Jagger waiting at the bottom looking perfectly put together—even with the stray streaks of blood here and there on their skin.

I offered an arched brow as I looked outside. We were only a few blocks away from where the vampires had tried to attack us, and it had been absolute chaos down there before we disappeared...but now there was nothing but silence. I mean, hadn't they been in the middle of a fight? Don't get me wrong, I was beyond grateful that they looked so at ease, but I still was confused. Not to mention that neither of them seemed bothered by overhearing Breaker and me.

"The threat has been dealt with," Jagger said. "No worries, little treasure."

"We should leave through the back exit, though," Gage said, his tone shifting slightly. I could feel the tension rolling through him.

"Why?" Breaker asked.

"It's a bit messy out there—the noise and scent of blood brought the fight a bit closer to here than I would have preferred," Gage grunted.

"We tried to give everyone a chance to leave, but some chose not to," Jagger added.

Tapping Breaker's chest, he let me slide down. I walked towards the door, but Gage appeared in front of me, stopping me. Worry filled my stomach as caution filled his gaze. I knew it wasn't about what he and Jagger had done, but how I would feel about it.

"The only way to kill a vampire is by beheading them..." Gage paused as my stomach tightened at the imagery that presented. "I know you don't like violence; you don't need to see it," he finished.

"They tried to attack us—tried to attack you three," I murmured, my eyes flickering over his shoulder as I swallowed hard. "I should look."

I knew my mates were known for being ruthless —heck, I'd been told multiple times that they were lethal and violent. I also knew the good they had in them and how much they loved me. If this was going to work, considering the danger we continued to find ourselves in, I needed to come to terms with those two things coexisting.

"Let her," Breaker said. I could feel through our bond that he didn't like the idea either, but he also understood. I think he knew exactly where I was coming from.

"Fuck," Gage muttered.

"Bexley—" Jagger didn't finish his sentence as I flashed towards the door, wanting to get it over with. I didn't make it out the doorway, though, my lips parting in surprise.

Messy. That was the word Gage had used to

describe the state of affairs out here...and he wasn't wrong. But it didn't explain why Gage and Jagger barely had any blood on them when the street was coated in it. My stomach churned uncomfortably as I took a steadying breath and stepped back.

For a singular moment, I was confused by my reaction. The physical one made sense, feeling queasy at the blood and decapitated bodies, but the confusion came with my mental reaction. I didn't blame my mates, nor did I think poorly of them that this is how it had ended. Mostly because I knew that if it could have ended with less violence, it would have.

They had done exactly that in the rogue lands—resolved things without using lethal force.

This had been necessary, clearly, and they had eliminated the threat to our small family.

"Cupcake." Gage's voice was tinged with an insecurity I wasn't used to. Turning from the door, I offered them a weak smile that seemed to confuse them more than anything.

"That—that is a lot of blood." I winced, then shook myself. "But let's keep moving. I don't want any more violence if we can avoid it."

Gage's eyes widened in surprise as Breaker chuckled, picking me up easily and walking us past Jagger, who was watching me with what might have been awe. I knew my reaction surprised my mates, but what they didn't realize was that I completely understood.

Because there was absolutely nothing I wouldn't do to protect them.

Chapter 13

Breaker Firespell

"I was expecting a different reaction," Gage said as we walked side by side, avoiding the bloodied street. It was the site of more than ten vampire deaths, including their unofficial leader.

Luckily, the rest had gotten the message and got the fuck out of dodge. The amount of blood and carnage really seemed like it belonged to a lot more than ten people, though. They must have *really* tried to attack Jagger and Gage. Usually we opted for a 'clean' death when it did have to occur, and *this* was the exact opposite of that.

Then again there wasn't much *clean* about ripping someone's head off.

"It's Bexley; she's always a surprise," I pointed out. My gaze followed her elegant frame, satisfaction hitting me hard when my gaze reached the mark on the back of her neck. My cock was still hard, remembering the sensation of filling her up with my cum, but more than anything there was contentment thrumming through our bond. It was impossible to ignore, and I knew that for the rest of our lives, I would be completely locked onto her.

Not that I hadn't been already, but before mating with her I'd managed some level of control—or at least pretended I had. Now it was a fucking lost cause, and the thoughts running through my head, possessive and dark, weren't reasonable and sure as fuck would scare her if she even had an inkling of them.

Probably.

Or maybe they wouldn't.

"I think we should head further into the neighborhood," Bexley said, turning around. She was walking ahead of me and Gage, next to Jagger, his hand protectively floating over her lower back. He was on high alert, as were Gage and me. Even now I could feel eyes on us, and I had no doubt that if we let our guard down for even a minute the vampires would take advantage of it.

I was honestly shocked they hadn't tried to attack us while we mated. It would have resulted in their immediate deaths for seeing my mate in such a state of perfection, but I was nonetheless surprised.

"Let's just keep an eye out; I don't trust how quiet it is," Gage said, his words underscored by the nervous energy moving through the bond that united us to Bexley.

Bexley nibbled her lip. "I don't like the idea of us being in danger, but I feel pulled towards the center of the city. Maybe it's my dragon trying to tell me something?"

That was completely possible.

"If that's where you want to go, then we will," I said, and she offered me a small smile. "But if a threat presents itself, we're going to get you out of here, okay? Your safety comes before everything."

"Deal," she said and leaned into Jagger. I had to control the urge to rip her from his arms. It wasn't anything against him; I just felt intensely possessive over the woman, especially now that I'd marked her. The taste of her blood was still on my tongue, and I had to fight the urge to drag her towards me, to bend her over so I could taste all of her...

"I'm just glad we haven't had any more confrontations," Gage said as we continued to walk. "Then again, I don't know how hierarchy and dominance work in vampire society."

"When we leave here we should send word to

Dracula of what happened, just so there aren't any misunderstandings," I murmured, keeping my gaze moving to all sides of our path.

"Agreed," Gage said.

As we made our way further into town, I continuously looked back towards Bexley, unable to help myself. My gaze moved down her curvy frame, along her hips, and I nearly groaned remembering how she looked pressed forward, braced on the window as I pummeled in and out of her.

She'd taken fucking all of me, every single inch of me, and then I'd filled her with so much cum that it was probably still dripping out of her...

My thoughts came to a full standstill, along with my feet, as something occurred to me that hadn't before. Or maybe it had and I'd been purposefully ignoring it...

"What's wrong? Hear something?" Gage asked, looking around.

"No, no." I shook my head and walked forward again, Gage keeping pace next to me, staring at me expectantly despite my denial. I knew I needed to say something...

"Is she on birth control?"

My question had Gage stumbling as he cast me a wide eyed look and glanced towards her. I didn't think for a moment that this was the first time the thought had crossed his head since they'd mated... then again, that had only been a few days ago. Fuck, we'd been so busy.

"No. No she is not."

"Fates," I mumbled, unable to help the sensation that worked over me—one that was so darkly possessive it almost worried me. The primal need I had to mark my mate with both my teeth and cum had made sense to me in the moment, but now my dragon was rolling under my skin as if thrilled with our revelation.

That Bexley wasn't protected in any way from us. That there had been nothing between us. That my seed could take root inside of her—

"Fuck," I groaned, stopping again as I laced my fingers behind my head and tried to shake my thoughts. "Gage, we should've said something—"

"Why?" Gage asked, a dark glint in his eye that I'd only seen a few times before, though almost always in reference to our mate.

"Because she should be aware—"

"Fuck." Gage seemed to shake himself from his initial reaction, running a hand through his hair in what I knew to be an anxious tell. "I know. I know you're right...I guess my thought process was that Bexley is fucking brilliant. She may not be consciously aware of the possibility, but I can't believe it hasn't crossed her mind. Either that or she was distracted like us...either way, though, she let us come inside of her, which means that on some level she wasn't worried about the possibility."

"That doesn't make any of this better," I growled in frustration. His logic wasn't off base, but who really cares about consequences in the heat of the moment? Once her head cleared, she might feel differently. I just felt off about this shit. Or maybe it was the desperate clawing joy in my throat at the concept of marking her so completely that she was carrying my damn baby that was making me feel almost fucking dizzy.

"We should say something," Gage agreed quietly before casting me a knowing look. "Does the idea of her being pregnant bother you?"

"Of course it fucking doesn't." I narrowed my gaze on him. "But she should know—"

"Know what?" Bexley called out, she and Jagger finally having noticed that we'd stopped. I didn't think she'd been listening to our conversation, which was good—we sounded like fucking nut jobs.

And if she was directly asking, we had to tell her.

Approaching her as Jagger continued to scope our surroundings, I tilted her chin up and examined her flushed face. Despite everything that had happened, there was a light that was so innate to Bexley that it still shone from every inch of her.

"We just realized we hadn't talked about using protection."

Jagger's eyes went comically wide as he snapped his head towards us, the thought clearly not having occurred to him either. Or, and here was a far better bet: all of us had been ignoring the thought because we wanted so badly to have nothing between us and our mate.

Our mate, who was staring at me with a soft curiosity but absolutely no surprise. She moved her gaze to Gage, then to Jagger, and back to me.

"I know," she said, her voice filled with uncertainty but also confusion, as if she didn't understand the problem. "I guess I just assumed...I mean, we're mates. Isn't that what mates do? They mate, and if it's forever, why use protection?"

I couldn't help the way I practically fucking mauled her as I kissed her hard enough that her knees broke, and she offered me a bewildered look as I pulled back. I ran a hand through my hair and tried to shake the insane thoughts in my head—namely how fucking thrilled I was at her words.

"So you don't mind? At all?" Jagger asked, his gaze darkening on her as she shrugged.

"I mean, I haven't been with anyone..."

"Neither have we, cupcake."

Relief filled Bexley's eyes, and she spoke softly, looking down. "I didn't want to ask, but I wondered."

"We've known you our entire life," I said. "Even a friendship with another woman would feel like cheating."

Bexley's cheeks flushed as she cast me a small smile. "I guess that's why I didn't think twice about it —I didn't want anything separating us."

I nearly groaned as I nodded, trying to keep myself from getting so damn hard.

"I fucking love that," Jagger rumbled, kissing the top of her head.

"That isn't the full reason I was concerned, though," I admitted, Gage offering me a concerned look that he tried to conceal from her. I had a feeling this was the part he was worried she'd freak out about.

"Oh?" She frowned.

"I didn't know if you'd thought about the possibility of getting pregnant."

The air whooshed out of her plush lips as her eyes widened. That had been the reaction I had been concerned about. Swallowing, Bexley offered a cute little frown as her nose crinkled in this damn adorable fashion—so fucking perfect.

"I..." Bexley exhaled. "No I guess I hadn't. I

mean...I had before, but everything has moved so fast, and I didn't know how that even worked—I know that some shifters need a mating heat to get pregnant, but outside of that my knowledge on the specifics is fairly limited, especially for dragons. I feel like all that talk was purposefully left out during school."

"Everything about mates was," Gage confirmed.

I rubbed her shoulder gently as I tucked a piece of hair behind her ear. "It's a small possibility. Dragons don't need a mating heat when they have established mating bonds, but it's something we should keep in mind. I don't want to scare you."

Especially since female storm dragons usually had multiple children at once. That concept was a bit insane to consider, if we were being honest. Not in a bad way, but I think all of us recognized that until we had this issue with Linan handled, no matter the possessive urge, it would be a dangerous time to have children.

Which gave me all the fucking motivation in the world to handle the bastard immediately.

Bexley nibbled her lip as she leaned back into Jagger, his grip on her possessive as I narrowed my eyes at how close he was to my fucking mark. "It's not that I'm scared, at all. I just hadn't thought about it. But the idea of being pregnant, of having a family with the three of you...I mean, I love that. I really love that."

And fuck did I love her.

"Well that makes all of this easy. You won't find any complaint from me." Jagger chuckled softly before murmuring something about 'handling Linan,' which made me know he was on the exact same page as myself.

Bexley's gaze moved to the two of us, and she seemed a bit unsure. "But how do you guys feel about it? Just because I'm okay with the idea of being pregnant doesn't mean—"

"More than okay with it, cupcake," Gage said, groaning and walking past our stopped group down the path. "In fact, so fucking okay with it that now I want to make it happen."

Jagger chuckled as I shook my head, unsurprised by his words. Bexley was, though—she made a surprised noise and looked up at me as we continued down the path, the tension from before and the serious nature of the conversation lightening.

"What about you?" she asked with honest concern.

"*Mo chuisle*," I mused softly, pulling her to a stop as they walked ahead, capturing her jaw and brushing my lips over hers. "You never need to ask that. I want what you want, and I would be fucking thrilled to get you pregnant."

"Breaker," she moaned softly.

"Let's go!" Gage growled from up ahead, causing Bexley to smile against my lips. As we turned to start walking, the smile remained.

"What?"

"Just thinking about how funny it would be to walk around campus pregnant," she said, her cheeks flushing. A groan rattled from my throat at the thought. I fucking loved that idea.

The image stuck with me as we walked for another ten minutes, before we found ourselves in a central park that stood out amongst the gothic stone and stormy skies. Bexley let out a pleased hum, and we kept her insulated between us as we stepped through the archway into the suburban oasis.

"Vampires," I said, nodding ahead to a group of them. Except they seemed young, maybe mid-teens, and when they saw us, only two out of the eight held their ground. The rest ran. I arched a brow as we made our way down the path to the two who remained. The girl stood from the bench, the boy next to her offering her a concerned look as he joined her.

"Hi there!" Bexley said, her cheerful tone making both of them jump.

"Hi?" The boy said, his gaze moving to the girl once again. "Danny, we should leave. Now. Those are dragons."

"I know." She squeezed his hand before fixing us with a gaze. "Why are you here?"

I appreciate the bold way in which she communicated, clearly feeling defensive at our presence. I had no intention of scaring either of them, so I kept quiet and let Bexley work her magic. If there was one thing she was amazing at—and there were about a million—it was getting others to understand her point and where she was coming from. She was just so damn passionate and understanding.

"We're looking for someone. Not a vampire—I suspect she's part witch and part shifter," Bexley said. "Very unique looking. Her name is Rebecca."

The girl's eyes widened and her shoulders slumped. "Why are you looking for her?"

The boy behind her wrapped an arm around her waist as he continued to stare at us with narrowed eyes. I offered him an amused look before redirecting my attention back to my mate, not wanting him to feel like I was trying to start some shit. I didn't need to have blood on my hands after the carnage we had already caused. Plus, much like Jagger and Gage, I was keeping tabs on the rest of the area around us.

"She's an old friend; I need to ask her something," Bexley explained simply.

The girl examined Bex's face before responding. "Well, unfortunately you're about a year too late. She was here—actually helped my family a few times with her potions," she said, her tone turning sad. "Although people were cruel about her appearance and the scales on her face."

"What happened to her?" Bexley asked, unease filtering through our bond.

"She left." The girl shrugged. "Literally just left one day."

"We think something scared her," the boy added. "The last we heard, she was heading to the portal—but like Danny said, that was a year ago."

Wonderful.

"Did she have a place here, by chance?" Bexley asked. "I would love to see it—she's left me clues in the past, and I'd like to check if she left any for me here."

Danny frowned. "I'm not sure if it's still intact. It's probably ransacked."

"That's okay, I'd still like to look," Bexley said. Danny looked up at the boy, and they seemed to come to a consensus. He sighed and nodded towards a nearby house.

"Luckily, it's not in anyone's territory—sort of no-

man's-land like the park. We can show you the way."
He tugged Danny into his side and began walking. I
allowed them some distance and kept my hand on
Bexley's lower back. As we walked through and out
of the park, I noticed a few more people making
themselves known, but they kept to themselves,
avoiding even looking at us.

When we arrived at the building, Danny and her
friend opened a broken door that led into a grand
foyer. They turned a right and went towards a door
that was left open, creaking in the subtle wind from
outside. The girl waved us over, and as my mate
approached the entryway to Rebecca's room, her
shoulders tensed. I had a feeling she was expecting to
find nothing, and I didn't blame her. Even from here
it was clear this place was empty and everything had
been stolen.

But her room in the rogue lands had looked simi-
larly empty, and that hadn't stopped the memory
spell from working on Bexley.

"You should step back." She told the two of
them. "Just in case."

The boy didn't hesitate in pulling Danny back,
and once Bex judged they were a safe distance away,
she walked through the door.

Or tried to.

"Fuck," I hissed as a thunderous boom sounded

outside, winds rattling the entire building. Bexley's knees broke as she gripped the doorway, and a pained noise came from her throat.

We tried to move forward to grab her, but she put up a hand to stop us. I wasn't fucking positive my dragon was going to have it any other way though. Then, all of the sudden the magic changed, and I could feel it rolling over our mate's skin as flashes and imagery played in front of my own eyes.

It wasn't clear like it undoubtedly was to Bexley, but I could see bits and pieces of Rebecca's journey. Jagger muttered a curse and put his head down in the face of the mounting pressure the magic was causing as Gage offered me a pained glance but otherwise stayed silent.

Then, as quickly as it began, it was over.

"Holy shit," the boy hissed as he pulled Danny back further. "What was that?"

I shrugged, trying to not portray how much the magic had affected me. "Magic."

Bexley wilted in the doorway, and I lifted her into my arms, turning to tell Danny and the boy, "You should get out of here. A power surge like that may attract the wrong people."

"Which means we need to leave as well," Gage said.

"I know where she went," Bexley murmured, melting into me.

"We can talk about it later, little treasure. You're about to pass out—"

"I don't want to forget." She forced her eyes open, and I came to a stop so we could all hear her.

"She went to..." Bexley's brow dipped as she ran a hand over her temple. Then her eyes began to flutter. "Natura. She went to Natura."

Shit. The fucking fae territory.

Chapter 14

Bexley Blackforge

"Natura isn't somewhere we can just travel to," Gage explained as we made our way out of the town in somewhat comfortable silence, Danny and her friend having walked most of the way with us. Well, not 'with us' because they were a few feet away, more escorts than companions—but I was thankful for it because it gave my brain some time to rest, not being able to talk about what I'd learned.

Not being able to analyze what it meant for us.

Rebecca's whereabouts and our plan moving forward—whatever it was—felt like something better left private, even if my assumption that Danny and her friend wouldn't really care was accurate. Although, she did say she knew her...

Either way, there was a lot to talk about, and this

new vision had been much clearer than the one Rebecca had left for me back in the rogue lands. I had a feeling that it had to do with time—only over a year had passed since this one had been placed, compared to the other which had been there for eight years before I found it.

"Why not?" I asked curiously, Breaker's bridal hold on me both possessive and secure as we made our way towards the portal. I wasn't positive how I felt about our trip to Sanguis, especially since we were already leaving.

Necessary, yes. But it also seemed to overcomplicate everything.

"The fae aren't like most species in our realm. Their society is far different than anything I've experienced, and that's just from meeting them in school," Jagger said.

"They also can't lie."

I blinked. "Like...at all?"

"Nope," Breaker said. "Which should make them trustworthy, but they're anything but. It's always fucking games with them."

"I wonder why Rebecca would go there."

"It's safe to an extent, because the fae don't interact much with the other realms. They sort of keep themselves in an isolated bubble," Gage explained.

"We need to think about what we want to do," I said, grimacing at the pounding in my head. "I can't think straight right now, though. That magic was so powerful. The other vision must have gotten diluted over time, but not this one."

"Close your eyes," Breaker suggested softly, and I rested my head against his large chest. The bond between us, between all my mates, was strong and thrumming with energy. It'd been only an hour or so ago, but it felt like a day had passed since Breaker had me in his arms and was marking me.

It had been such an intense need, to have all of him, and while I'd been confused and insecure about the seriousness of our relationship when they brought up protection, *I was no longer confused.* At all. In fact, I'd never been so freakin' positive about how we all felt about our love and our future. It was a huge relief, and I found myself wanting to shout how much I loved them.

I needed to tell Jagger in private first, though. I'd known it for some time, especially with all of my memories flooding back, but I wanted to see his eyes darken to charcoal as I admitted just how crazy I was about him.

The best part? I knew he felt just as intensely.

At some point during our walk to the portal, I fell asleep and was pulled into a dream, memories that

I'd been spelled to forget beginning to resurface. Many of them weren't substantial enough to be more than flashes and images, but some were clearer and more complete than others—and all of them had to do with my mates.

"He shouldn't be here." Breaker's voice was a lot more serious than before. I tilted my head up to see him glaring at a wolf shifter I didn't recognize. He looked around our age, though.

"His mom lives here," Gage said. "It's his dad who isn't allowed here."

"Still don't like it," Jagger murmured, siding with Breaker.

The shifter was walking with my mom and Carol, the woman who'd been living with us for a few years now. "Bexley, honey, this is Carol's son, Fletcher."

"Nice to meet you!" I perked up and offered him a small smile. His returning smile faded, though, when Jagger's hand intertwined with mine, his gaze moving to Gage and Breaker. The four of them seemed to have a weird conversation through looks alone.

I didn't understand how they freakin' did that.

"Fletcher," Carol warned softly. He snapped his gaze away and looked up at his mom, his ears turning pink.

"It's only natural. They're all alphas; even at this age they can't help it," my mom said, her voice filled with understanding. "Although this is a celebration."

"We won't fight," Breaker promised, and my mom offered him an affectionate look. It was a good promise for him to make, because one time Breaker had an issue with another boy around our age, and that hadn't been resolved nearly as peacefully.

At least from what I'd heard. I hadn't been around when they'd gotten into a fight. I had been worried about my friend, though, and had gone to see him the minute I found out about it.

"Thank you for letting me come here, even if it's a short amount of time," Fletcher said with such sincerity that my mom's eyes filled with emotion as she motioned for him to follow her. I could feel everyone's eyes on us, and I had a feeling that this boy being here was a big deal.

I briefly remembered the man who'd tried to bring Carol back home with him—Linan Clanguard. My dad said to stay away from him...did the same apply to her son? I didn't think so. Yet I couldn't help the queasy feeling in my stomach at the idea that Linan might come here to get Fletcher, too, even if it was just to pick him up when his visit was over.

My parents wouldn't allow that. Right?

. . .

"Cupcake."

I blinked my eyes open and found myself staring into Gage's deep green gaze.

"I just had the weirdest dream," I murmured, sitting up in his lap and finding that we were in...a car? Fates. Had I slept through portalling? I must have been absolutely exhausted. I blinked in confusion, noticing the busy streets and large buildings that signaled we were back in our territory.

"About what?" Jagger asked from his seat next to Breaker. The inside of the car was similar to a limo in the sense that there was a partition between the driver and us, and the seats weren't facing forward. Instead they lined the walls like a couch so we could talk easily.

"Meeting Fletcher when he came to visit his mom."

Breaker let out a hum of understanding, clearly recalling the memory as well.

"I wish all my memories would be that clear, especially about *that* night. I know there's more to it than my brain is showing me."

"Don't force it." Gage kissed my shoulder. "It'll come when it's supposed to. I remember meeting Fletcher that first time, but I don't think any of us understood just how messy the situation was with

Carol—I don't think our parents ever told us why she was staying at your estate to begin with."

Now we knew, though.

I nibbled my lip in thought. "I know we don't have a plan, but I don't think we can just go back to campus without knowing what we're going to do next, especially since we have a lead on where Rebecca is."

"I agree," Breaker said. "I think we should spend the night in one of our territories and decide in the morning where to go from there. Knowing where she was a year ago is huge, and considering she was in vampire territory for almost seven years, I presume she wouldn't have moved on from her new place yet."

"And that's not even including the fact that the fae territory is far easier to hide in compared to Sanguis," Jagger agreed.

"I'm glad we have tabs on Linan right now, but you're right, cupcake—it doesn't feel right to just head back to campus," Gage said. "The idea of a threat out there, unhandled, will bother me until my dragon forces a shift and I try to leave campus myself."

"That sounds painful," I commented, making him chuckle. After a long moment, I said, "Alright, let's go to one of the estates. Which is the closest?"

"To the city and portal? Probably mine," Breaker said, his eyes darkening. "But it will mean seeing my parents."

"They may have some insight of their own, and it would be an easy way to contact the other parents as well without going to each estate," Jagger pointed out.

"And if we do plan to go to the fae territory, they may have advice on what we need to do to prepare," Gage agreed.

"I'm excited to see your home," I told Breaker, moving off Gage's lap and towards him. The other two were talking about contacting their own parents, but I was more than happy snuggled on my mate's lap.

I knew he was hesitant about going home, but I wanted to learn more about him. See where he grew up. I wanted to know everything about him, and not just through long-forgotten memories.

"My home is with you." He brushed his lips against my forehead. "With that being said, I'm excited to bring you there and show my mate off."

I blushed as I tilted my head back and got a soft kiss from him. Melting into it, I pulled back after a long moment and laid my head on his shoulder to watch the city pass by. Breaker's soothing hand on my back had me in a relaxed, lulled state as I looked skyward at the bright crisp sky, and I knew without a doubt that it was colder than it had been this morning.

I wasn't positive what time it was, but if I had to guess, it was early evening—or maybe not even evening yet, but late afternoon. It had been such an odd day—

My stomach grumbled. Loudly.

Groaning in embarrassment, I tucked my head down. Breaker chuckled, but there was a tense edge to it. Gage cursed. "When did you last eat? Shit, Bex, we should've packed something."

"I'm good," I promised. "Just embarrassed."

"Here," Jagger said, handing me a bag of trail mix. "It's not much, but I grabbed some from the hotel just in case."

"Good thinking," Gage said, relaxing back into his seat as I opened the bag. With my mates appeased, I ate my trail mix quietly, keeping my eyes on the changing landscape. We went from an urban sprawl of concrete and glass to the tree-lined streets of small towns before arriving at the country estate that belonged to the Firespell family.

Despite a lack of memories, a sense of familiarity crawled over me, reminding me that I had been here many times before.

The home was simplistic in nature, but not in a

bad way—just beautiful and stately without all the extra stuff. There wasn't any fancy landscaping, or lighting as the sky grew darker. Just a massive stone mansion that produced a glow that seemed to warm the land around it. I smiled, having a feeling that I was going to like Breaker's house—mainly because I knew it would reveal so much about him.

"It's beautiful," I told him honestly as the car began its journey up the winding driveway.

"It's something," he grumbled.

I pulled back. "We can go somewhere else." I knew home wasn't his favorite place, but I didn't want him to be truly uncomfortable.

"It's okay, *mo chuisle*. Just know how my parents can be—very opinionated about shit that is none of their business. Then again, you're with me, so they'll probably act completely differently."

"I'll protect you from them," I said, completely serious.

He chuckled and flashed me a gorgeous smile. "I believe that, Bexley."

When the car pulled to a stop, I inhaled and looked towards the large doors that were opening in response to our arrival. Breaker's parents were already there to greet us, and when I looked back at my mate and the apprehension painted on his face, I wondered if maybe I really would have to protect him.

Chapter 15

Bexley Blackforge

"Bexley, it's so good to see you again." My eyes widened at the sweet sentiment as I returned the tight hug that Mrs. Firespell gave me. I hadn't known what to expect, but the more than welcoming reception was actually really nice—and Breaker seemed ten times more relaxed now that we were in the door. Even his dad seemed happy to see us.

"I wish I'd known ahead of time that you were going to come," his dad said to my mates as I pulled back from the hug. "We would have prepared a celebration."

"We didn't even know we would be," I explained, turning towards him. "We just came back from Sanguis."

"What?!" Mrs. Firespell screeched, holding me

at arm's length so she could inspect me for damage. I honestly hadn't expected this type of concern over me, but my surprise was nothing compared to Breaker's as he stared at his mom with wide eyes.

"It's sort of a long story," I hedged.

"I think we have a lot to explain, and some questions," Breaker said.. "But first, she needs to eat, and we need to shower—Jagger and Gage have blood on them."

And I had Breaker *on* and *in* me. I nearly blushed at that thought.

"Not ours," Jagger immediately assured them. Breaker's mom relaxed, having gone even more tense.

"Let me show you to your room. You have to stay the night, I won't accept no for an answer." Mrs. Firespell gently led me towards a hallway, staying true to her word and not even giving us a minute to discuss it. "Let's have dinner in the library after the four of you wash up, and then you can tell us everything."

"Wouldn't it be better to start with the story?" Breaker's dad asked. I got the impression the man was sort of impatient in general.

"Are you sure none of you need medical attention?" Mrs. Firespell asked, completely ignoring Mr.

Firespell's question. He looked almost like he was sulking but otherwise moved on.

"Totally fine," Gage assured her.

"I'm good," I promised. "Breaker got me out of there while the two of them handled the vampires who attacked."

She looked at my neck for just a moment, her gaze quickly darting away. "I smelled blood on you, so I worried."

My cheeks were now absolutely bright red.

"That isn't from fighting," I murmured, wanting to assure her but also wanting to crawl into a hole.

"Right." She nodded, her ears turning red, and I felt a bit comforted that I wasn't the only one who found this scenario awkward. You know, like her seeing her son's mating mark and knowing exactly how it'd gotten there.

If it had been Celine I was talking to about this it would have been a little bit better—still totally embarrassing, but less for sure. I just didn't know Breaker's mom that well.

After a long moment, she recovered. "Anything specific for dinner?"

"Pasta would be awesome," I said before I could stop myself, my stomach speaking for me. But my embarrassment clearly wasn't enough to stop me from adding, "And cupcakes."

Finally, my brain wrested control of my words and I quickly added, "But I totally understand if you don't have—"

"My chef is going to be thrilled." She laughed as we turned the corner towards a set of large dark doors. "We rarely eat anything but meat and vegetables. I can't wait to tell him."

"As long as it's not a big deal," I added, not wanting her to feel inconvenienced.

"Never," she assured me, moving on to the next topic. "I feel like we didn't get to talk at the ball. I'm really glad you're here."

"I'm glad to be here too." I squeezed her arm, feeling relief that my instincts had been right about this. Maybe Breaker's parents were just the type of people who felt like they had to portray a certain image in front of others, because at home they seemed far different.

Or I could be totally wrong. I needed to talk to my mate and make sure he was comfortable with all of this.

"Here we go!" She turned towards the boys. "This suite is Breaker's, but it has guest suites that can be reached through it. You should find anything you need in the closets and vanities, but if you do need anything, please let me know."

"And we will have dinner brought to the library,"

Mr. Firespell said, before adding hopefully, "Where you'll tell us what you were doing in Sanguis?"

"Give it a break," Mrs. Firespell huffed. "Just be glad our son and his mate came to visit, will you?"

"I am glad." Mr. Firespell frowned and looked at Breaker. "You know I'm glad to see you and Bexley, right? It's great to see you."

I offered a smile as Breaker nodded, his gaze only betraying the slightest hint of tension.

"Come on," Mrs. Firespell said on a sigh, dragging her husband away as Breaker opened the door to his suite.

What lay inside was quite different from the rest of the house, which had a medieval feel with its stone walls and tapestries. This room was modern in comparison, dark, masculine furniture positioned around a lit fireplace. Even better, the room smelled exactly like Breaker. I inhaled happily and walked inside, noticing that someone had already set out a light snack as well as some refreshments for us. They must've been told to bring them the moment we'd been spotted heading down the driveway.

The Firespells really were excited to have us here.

"I'm going to go shower!" I turned towards my mates to find Jagger almost right behind me, catching me with a hand to my hip. Gage and Breaker, on the other hand, were opening windows and settling into the space.

"I wish I could join you." Jagger nipped my ear, and I shivered under his touch.

"You should," I said softly but boldly.

"I can't, little treasure. I don't trust myself to not take it farther than we have, especially when my dragon knows another mate has marked you. My control is limited right now, to say the least."

"Oh." I nibbled my lip. "I'm sorry—"

"Don't apologize." He brushed my nose. "It's my dragon being an asshole. Plus, I don't want to kill Breaker when he gets all possessive about his mark on the back of your neck."

"You're not wrong," Breaker muttered, the corners of his lips quirking up.

Gage appeared next to us and gently prodded me towards the shower. "Come on, cupcake. I need you to shower so we can get you some damn food."

"I am hungry," I admitted as he walked me towards a set of double doors. I stepped through them and instantly found myself surprised by the amount of products on the vanity. Sure, I'd brought a fair amount of things in my bag, but this was really thoughtful.

"Shower," Gage reminded me. I could feel

through our bond just how anxious he was over me being hungry.

After turning on the shower and hearing the door click shut, I shed my adorable outfit and slipped into the hot water. A relieved groan left my lips as the shower filled with steam and I relaxed under the stream as it massaged my shoulders.

It didn't take long to clean up, taking care to not press on my mating mark which was still fairly tender, and afterwards I stayed under the water just a bit longer, savoring it. Eventually though, realizing everyone else needed a turn, I got out and pulled on a robe, loving the soft material against my skin.

Brushing my hair and then my teeth, I left my golden locks down and towel dried them before walking towards a large closet attached to the bathroom. I'd only expected to find Breaker's clothes, but in addition there was a rack in the center of the room with the sort of comfortable, smock-like dresses that I'd seen his mom wear twice now.

I chose a dress in pale blue then sorted through a bag of undergarments, removing the tags and getting dressed. I didn't have shoes but figured I could pull back on my boots or something, so I grabbed some fuzzy socks before returning to the bathroom.

I wouldn't lie, I pouted a bit when none of them were in the shower. It's not that I'd wanted to walk in on that...but I also wouldn't have minded in the least. Apparently they'd showered elsewhere, because all three of them were changed and squeaky clean when I entered the main room.

"You look beautiful," Breaker said.

"Thanks," I said, even though that probably wasn't the case, especially with how it hung on my body. But I loved how sweet he was nonetheless.

"Are you sure you're comfortable with staying?" Gage asked Breaker.

"Yeah." Breaker sighed. "My dad's a piece of shit —or was—but I honestly haven't spent a lot of time with him since starting school. Even on summers off I was constantly traveling, between trying to leave notes for Bexley"—I smiled at that—"and helping train shifters in our territory. With that being said, he appears to have changed a lot in the past year or two, and I'm not sure why."

"Your mom seems sweet," I observed.

A thoughtful look crossed his face. "She does. She was also like that in private for a lot of my childhood. It's my dad I've had a huge issue with—but like I said, he seems different, so I'm willing to give him a chance."

"Not that he deserves one," Jagger added. "I don't give a shit what he labeled it as, the training he put you through was bullshit."

I nodded in agreement. Despite thinking that his scars only made him more handsome, I wasn't a fan of how he'd gotten them—intense training that no kid should have been put through, at the hand of his father.

Of course, right then, in the middle of an important conversation, my freakin' stomach rumbled.

I had never seen them move faster, a giggle escaping as Jagger picked me up because I wasn't walking fast enough. I loved the tight hold on me though and easily melted into it, my head resting on his shoulder as we made our way through the stone hallways.

"I don't have shoes," I pointed out, wiggling my toes in my socks.

Gage flashed me a wide smile. "Good—means we can carry you everywhere."

Only a few minutes later we approached two large gilded doors in black iron and gold that were partly open, a warm light radiating from within the library. Wiggling down from Jagger's hold, I followed Breaker in and was greeted by the smells of an absolute feast.

"Food just arrived!" Mrs. Firespell exclaimed. Breaker's father looked up from a book he was reading, immediately closing it and sitting forward eagerly.

"Sit, I'll make you a plate," Gage murmured, so I sat down on a velvet couch nearby. I could feel through our bond how much he wanted to take care of me, and I had absolutely no problem with that.

I smiled happily as Breaker sat next to me and draped a blanket over my lap, and Jagger grabbed me a cup of hot tea that I placed on the end table. I heard Breaker's dad say something, but I was far too captivated with the massive plate of food that Gage put in front of me. I thanked him and then dug in, appreciating the array of pasta and meat they'd prepared. There were even some sweets, and the plate of cupcakes across the room was calling my name.

Luckily for Gage, who would probably tell me to eat 'real food' first, I wasn't in the mood for them just yet. Instead I began to cut up my steak as Breaker spoke up, narrowly avoiding another impatient remark from his father. "She's going to eat while we explain what's been going on," he said. "*Mo chuisle*, add anything I forget?"

"Absolutely," I assured him.

But he didn't forget a thing. I was enraptured by his detailed descriptions and insightful observations about what we'd been through. From explaining the visions I had about that night and what happened in the city, along with our attempts to find Rebecca, to even learning about the prophecy, he covered it perfectly. I had to assume he'd practiced his observational skills in training because it was really impressive.

"So Sanguis was useful, to an extent," Breaker concluded, "but it means that now we have to decide if we want to follow Rebecca's path into fae territory."

"I wish we'd been alerted of the meeting sooner." Mr. Firespell's gaze was dark. "Clanguard knows his limits, and to come to all four of you at school is inexcusable."

"We wanted to handle it on our own, especially if this is going to be an ongoing problem with him," Gage explained.

"Although we have to assume that his decision to create problems now has nothing to do with territory and everything to do with—"

"Bexley." Mrs. Firespell interrupted him with her conclusion and folded her hands, her gaze going distant. "You are right on the mark about Carol. She was from the same village as your mom, and when Linan went too far one night and not only assaulted her but also threatened to hurt the kids if she didn't comply with his demands, she tried to remove herself from the equation. She knew Linan wouldn't hurt their sons—the bastard and his pack always targeted women when they hurt people."

"And he's pissed at my mom because of that? So with me returning he's upset?" I asked.

"Something like that. I also don't believe he wants the rogue lands. I think he wanted to goad you into action," Mr. Firespell said. "Which worked to an extent, but I don't think he knows about Rebecca. If Linan is responsible for the slaughter that night, he'll be extinguished from this territory. That was one of the most brutal and gruesome nights Trabea has ever seen."

"If he'd known about Rebecca escaping, he would've hunted her down," Mrs. Firespell agreed. "He's temperamental, but with age he's become very focused on tying up all of his loose ends. Which leads me to believe that he may be doing worse things than we're even aware of."

"Do you think any of it could be connected to the prophecy?" Gage asked. I think it was something we were all thinking about. It was possible that Clanguard didn't even know about the prophecy, but if he did...well, I could see why it would cause him to panic.

"We didn't even know about the prophecy until you just told us." Mr. Firespell frowned. "So he would have had to have someone on the inside in order to know about it. It's clear your parents were concerned enough to keep it quiet."

Crap. Well, that sort of negated that, unless there had been a spy in our home.

"Although..." Mrs. Firespell stood, looking over the tall shelves that lined the library walls. "You guys are jogging my memory about something your mom gave me, Bexley. I don't remember when, and I assumed it'd been a mistake when I found it in the stack of books she lent me, but by the time I went to ask her about it...well, everything had happened and it wasn't important anymore."

"What was it?" I sat up on my knees as she searched the shelves. It was hard not to get lost in a surge of sadness every time someone mentioned my parents' death, so instead I focused on the mystery at hand.

"Here we go!" she exclaimed after another minute of searching, carrying the book back to our group. "This is a catalog of everything the Blackforge seers predicted. We don't use that type of magic in our clan, so it held no interest for me, but now..."

She placed the book in my hands, and I felt a wave of magic roll over my fingers. I didn't know what type of magic it was, but it felt friendly, the leather cover warming in my hands—

The book snapped open.

I watched in surprise, my mates tensing, as the pages began to glow gold. They fluttered in a ghost wind, turning to one of the last pages in the book.

Other than the seer's name and the date written at the top, it contained only one thing—*the prophecy*, commanding attention from the center of the page.

When the time comes that four lines are united by one heir who threatens everything created in the darkness, the territory will be made anew, reborn in the ashes of the cursed pack.

My hearing went static as Jagger read it out loud for Breaker's parents. My chest tightened as my stomach sank in realization.

I didn't know how he found out, but if he even thought for a minute that the 'cursed pack' was in reference to his...it was more than enough reason for Clanguard to attack my family. To view us as a threat that could only be eliminated through mass slaughter.

I was the reason for that slaughter—the Flash Clan's death was on my hands.

Chapter 16

Jagger Silvershade

"This will be good, I need this," Bexley said as we left breakfast in the Firespell's kitchen. I nodded at her assessment, knowing that she was saying it more to herself than anything, and kept a hand against her back in case she needed to lean into me more.

Last night had been rough in so many ways.

The first reason was obvious—*the prophecy*. The shade of white that Bexley's face had turned would live in my mind rent free for a very long time—I'd been worried she was about to pass out right on the spot. Then when she told us she thought her entire clan's death was on her hands because of how Clanguard interpreted the prophecy... It was bullshit. She wasn't responsible for his actions nor what had happened, but try as I might I couldn't convince her of that, and she'd fallen asleep in my arms still tormented by the thought.

My little treasure was so damn caring and loving, filled with compassion, that having that type of weight on her shoulders would severely affect her.

Which was why the rest of the night was increasingly difficult. Dreams had tormented her through the early hours of the dawn, causing her to twist and turn, not allowing for more than a few hours of solid sleep before she sat up gasping in panic. It was so bad that Gage, Breaker, and I had stayed up on shifts for most of the night to comfort her.

I wasn't positive that it had helped, so I was trying our next best option. Flying.

"The others will be joining us soon," I assured her as we walked through a long stone hallway. Gage and Breaker were updating the other clan leaders on a conference call, and while my parents probably wanted to hear from me, I was more interested in focusing on my mate.

Plus, I didn't want Bexley to be part of a conversation that would include a discussion about that night—the night she was now blaming herself for. At least not yet.

"I feel bad. I kept all of you up most of the night." She frowned, leaning further into me.

"I'm just worried you didn't rest enough," I

replied, smoothing a hand over her wavy hair. She nodded in agreement, and I hated that her naturally upbeat demeanor was being weighed down by Clanguard's bullshit.

It made me want to find the bastard—

I stilled those thoughts. Bexley would be able to sense my growing anger, and I didn't want her to think it was towards her.

My chest relaxed slightly as we walked out into the pavilion, Bex smiling up at the cloudy skies above. I didn't think it was going to storm today, but the energy was there, and I could feel it fueling both of our dragons.

"I haven't shifted without jumping before," she said, biting down on her plush lip. "Well, except that one time—"

A rumble escaped my chest. She was talking about when she'd been attacked. *Fucking Ioan.*

"I just don't know how to do it on purpose. I mean, I do, but now I'm nervous." She huffed, the adorable action showing her frustration.

"Focus on the flame and pull on our bonds. I can also shift first if you think it'll make your dragon more eager to get up in the air."

"Yes," Bexley said immediately. "That's a great idea."

"Alright. Back up, little treasure." I pressed a kiss

to her forehead and jogged to the center of the open-air pavilion. Looking skyward, I pulled on the roaring inferno in the center of my chest and—

I exploded up into the air.

It felt like second nature to me, but I focused more on the transformation this time, trying to view it the same way Bexley would. The way our skin seemed to burn away to reveal scales. The way our bodies morphed and grew larger, going airborne as massive wings pushed out from our shoulders. The vicious sound that left my throat, a roar that rattled the Firespell estate windows and caused Bexley to let out a small laugh.

Our mate. Our mate was happy seeing us shifted —and we wanted her up in the air with us.

Circling around, I watched as she went towards the same takeoff point I'd used and looked skyward. I worried for a long moment that she was going to psych herself out—because I knew she was more than capable of doing it. But soon that wasn't a problem.

Bexley transformed into a sleek obsidian scaled creature and blasted into the sky surrounded by golden flames that flickered bronze and silver. It was glorious, and her responding roar to mine had something settling in my chest. This was *exactly* how we were meant to be.

I didn't hesitate to lead her away from the estate, knowing that she needed a break—knowing that she needed a release from thinking—and there was no better way to do that than in dragon form. It helped that I was very familiar with this territory, and as we soared above tall trees and through open agricultural fields, I let Bexley take the lead. I knew she was pushing harder than normal and it would no doubt exhaust her, but I could also feel the contentment and happiness flowing through our bond.

It was fucking glorious.

When she darted upwards towards the sky and her magic pulsed, I wondered briefly what she was doing—but then her magic slammed into me and I saw. Not just saw, but was thrust fully into the memory Bex was experiencing.

"Mom! Jagger and I just finished flying—"

Bexley came to a hard stop, skidding against the stone floor of the balcony, as my hand shot out to catch her shoulders. I was watching from a distance, and it caught me off guard seeing the two of us together, but as kids. I had my own memories of our time together, and seeing one in the third person like this was...odd. Very odd.

"Maybe we should come back?" the younger

Surge

version of me asked Bexley as we both stared at her
mother, who didn't even look up to greet us. Instead,
she was fully focused on the cloaked woman in front
of us. Their conversation was intense and filled with a
heavy sense of dread.

As I walked towards their table, I stood next to
Bexley's mom and realized the cloaked figure was
Rebecca. The two of us hesitated in the door, but I
turned my attention to the conversation at hand,
knowing there was something important to be heard
here. After all, magic didn't interfere like this unless it
was necessary.

"They're coming. I don't know when, but
they're coming," Rebecca said darkly. "You need to
run."

"We are not running," Bexley's mom hissed.

"I'm not sure we can survive what I've seen,"
Rebecca said, her face filled with remorse. "I'm not
sure she'll survive."

"Don't," Bexley's mom spit out, standing. "We'll
talk about this later, but surrender, hiding—those are
not options."

She wasn't even willing to speak on the other
element, and I didn't blame her. I had a feeling
Rebecca was talking about Bexley's death.

"Sorry honey!" Her mom plastered on a smile,
moving her gaze towards the doorway, and walked

around the desk. "Let's go grab a snack and you two can tell me about your flight."

The doors closed, and I was left with just Rebecca, who was...staring right at me.

My chest seized up, feeling a weird surge of adrenaline. Was it fear? Not exactly, but it was some-thing. Before she could say anything, her mouth opening to do just that, I was pulled from the dream—

A pained whimper from my mate had my eyes snapping open as I groaned, realizing that I had not only shifted back but that my shoulder and face were covered in dirt. Bexley was curled on top of me, crying into my chest. I looked around, grasping my bearings and realized we had crashed into a fucking field...but I had caught her? Thank fuck for that.

"Jagger." Bexley snapped her gaze up, eyes filled with tears. "I don't understand. She knew—she knew something was going to happen and did nothing—"

"I don't think she did *nothing*." I sat up and pulled her against me, trying to soothe her anguish. "In fact, I think this memory was held back for a specific reason—it's tainted in Rebecca's magic. She looked right at me in it. "

"I saw." Bexley groaned and pressed her head

against my neck. "I just don't understand. I don't know what to do—"

My mate froze and inhaled, something odd settling over her. I felt her magic flare, and when her gaze snapped up, I saw a strength radiating from her that distinctly reminded me of her mother in that memory.

"I know what to do." Bexley ran a hand under her eyes to wipe away the tears. "We need to find Rebecca—no matter the cost and missing school—we need to find her. We need confirmation and the full truth of what happened."

Before I could respond, she let out a shaky exhale. "More so, if Clanguard was the reason for this genocide and it was because of the prophecy, I can't let that go unchecked. I don't know what I'm going to do, but I am going to fix this, Jagger."

"I believe you, little treasure." I cupped her face and examined the softness there, mixed with a strength that I loved seeing in her. "And I will be here with the others every step of the way. No matter what."

Bexley nodded sharply, and while I saw determination, I also saw something else. Something that wasn't characteristic of my mate, but had my blood fucking pumping—the need for vengeance.

If that was what my little treasure wanted, she was damn well going to get it.

* * *

It had been a few hours since taking the long way home, allowing Bexley some time to her own thoughts. The minute we landed to find the other two waiting for us, it was clear she was feeling far better. More determined and more focused, announcing that we were leaving for the fae territory tonight.

And who the hell were we to say no?

Well, except that we were her concerned fucking mates, and she wanted to go into a foreign territory that wasn't exactly the safest. But we kept that conversation between us as I updated them on every-thing that had happened with the vision and Bexley's realization on how she wanted to handle going forward. I was unsurprised to find that the other two supported her idea but were as concerned as myself.

Which is why we sat talking about how to ensure her safety, giving a heads up to the territory ruler that we'd be visiting to avoid conflict. We handled all of this, as well as updating the parents, while Bexley took a long shower and got ready to leave.

Most of our items were packed up when she came out of the bathroom, dressed and ready to go.

"Shit," Breaker murmured as I looked over her soft green dress that had long sleeves and an ankle length skirt embroidered with delicate flowers. That alone I could have dealt with...but paired with pink fucking combat boots and a pink and yellow corset over the top? A corset that highlighted her perfect fucking curves and drew my attention to her cleavage? One that had me imagining placing my mark on the swell of her breasts—

This outfit was going to be a fucking problem.

"How do I look?" Bexley did a small turn as a rumble broke from my throat.

"Fucking edible," I muttered. She practically giggled at the clear pain in my voice before turning and showing off her long locks and the pink bow there. *Fucking hell.* I didn't understand why I found that attractive, except that maybe I imagined taking it out of her hair and wrapping it around her wrists.

"Thank you." She flashed a smile. "I thought it was fun. Plus, Mrs. Firespell said that it was a bit more old fashioned over there—that they had an antiquated style."

That was an understatement.

"So this is your fault," Gage growled at Breaker—

who shrugged, looking absolutely unbothered by the accusation.

"I don't normally feel like I have curves, but I'm starting to see the appeal of corsets." Bexley motioned to the bodice, drawing my gaze to her cleavage once again as I noticed a blush creep across her skin at our attention. "I mean, seriously—it's pretty great. As long as it isn't too tight—then it wouldn't be nearly as fun. Breathing is important."

I barked out a laugh, unable to help myself as her eyes sparkled at my amusement.

"Maybe a jacket—"

"No, then I'll be hot!" Bexley sang and waltzed towards the door. "Come on, let's go to the portal—I want to try to open it myself again."

Something I was still getting over.

Gage walked ahead with her and Breaker trailed next to me, his amusement fading into concern. "She seems like she's done a one-eighty. Should we be concerned?"

"Yes and no," I breathed out. "She's not hiding it or trying to ignore how she's feeling, so that's good. I think she's just redirecting her anger."

"I suppose that's good," Breaker grunted. "At least Natura isn't as outwardly violent as Sanguis. Just have to worry about getting pulled into shit that we don't have time for."

"I'm hoping that since we've already told them we're coming, the Crown Prince will mediate any of those issues for the sake of keeping the peace." And if he didn't, we could always shift and fly the fuck away.

"I wish you weren't leaving already," Mrs. Firespell said from up ahead. She and her husband were standing at the front door to see us out, our belongings taken by estate workers to be packed in the car.

"Not used to that," Breaker admitted, no doubt in reference to his parents' display of emotion. "You know he apologized today?"

I arched a brow as he continued to explain. "I think she laid into him about how he acts, specifically towards me, because he tried to talk to me about my training as a kid—"

In a ridiculously blunt yet awkward manner, no doubt.

"—and then apologized, saying that he'd been trying his best to prepare me for the world. That he didn't realize he was doing anything wrong, but now knows different."

"Well that is progress." I sighed, still thinking the guy was a piece of crap for putting his kid through military training. At the same time, the fact that he was not only apologizing but making attempts to change was a good sign. I was still reserving judgment, though, until he actually followed through.

"I have a feeling what prompted Mom to say something because then he mentioned that when I have kids, he doesn't want me to make the same mistake."

I barked out a laugh. If there was one thing that unified the three moms, it was excitement over grandbabies. Of course they would never say that to us, especially since our mating announcement was so new and we hadn't had a formal ceremony yet, something akin to a wedding...but I heard them talking about it pretty much the entire time we were at the Bronzeheart estate after the ball.

I didn't mind it one fucking bit, and neither did Bexley, it seemed.

"You'll never be like him," I assured my friend, and he shot me a thankful glance before we reached his parents. I was glad that he and his father seemed to be making amends, but my dragon was naturally protective, and while they were all 'alphas' in their own right, I considered these men—my brothers, essentially—to be part of my flight.

After goodbyes, I scooped Bexley into my arms and kissed her nose. When I pulled back, she smiled up at me. "Do you think I'll like Natura?"

"Yeah, I actually think you will, little treasure."

Chapter 17

Bexley Blackforge

"Cupcake, don't you dare."

My scowl slipped further onto my lips as I walked along the stone path leading right out of the portal—the portal my mates hadn't let me even *attempt* to freakin' open. Which was why I was, in fact, sporting a pout. And I didn't feel bad about it at all.

Plus, not that I would fully admit to it, but the lighthearted teasing was allowing me to feel a bit more relaxed after the intensity of this morning and last night. A night filled with dreams that had left me both exhausted and on edge.

But I totally wasn't going to focus on that right now. Nope, not at all. Not even the slightest.

Pulling myself from that particular pathway of

thoughts, I briefly glanced around as I walked ahead, the heavy foliage I was now surrounded by not giving me a clear indication of what this new territory was like. But I would admit—it smelled beautiful. Like rich soil that had been soaked in a heavy rainfall.

As I turned to look back at my mates, I noticed the portal behind them shimmering before closing completely, leaving only what appeared to be a natural arch from two trees leaning towards one another. It was beautiful but simple, and if I hadn't just stepped through it, I wouldn't have suspected its true nature.

Our territory had always embraced nature, most likely because our magic did. That even extended to the city, at least from what I'd seen so far, where a lot of green spaces and bodies of water had been left alone in its development. But it was clear, even from the small bit of this territory I'd seen, that they'd embraced nature on a completely different level.

"Why is she pouting? I don't like that she's doing that," Jagger said, confusion and tension filling his voice. There was a rigidness to his entire frame as he stared at me in concern—and I felt bad, I wouldn't lie, but not completely bad because it was also kind of adorable that he was getting so worked up over an expression on my face.

Plus, he had literally opened the portal! Hadn't even freakin' asked me if I had wanted to try it out.

"*Mo chuisle* is upset because we didn't let her open the portal," Breaker said, translating my frustration.

"You didn't even ask me to," I huffed. "What if I wanted to open it? Heck, I *did* want to, but you just did it without asking."

"You need to save your energy. I don't deny that it's amazing that you can do it on your own, but it could easily drain you and I have no idea what we're going to face in this territory. You may need your magic," Gage reminded me gently, catching up to walk beside me. I offered him a narrow look before resuming my sulking.

"The three of you get to do cool stuff all the time," I grumbled, stepping over a fallen tree. Afternoon sunlight broke through the canopy and hit me across the face, so I shielded my eyes as I continued. "Then I find out I can do one thing that no one else can easily and you don't even ask me to do it again!"

"Most people don't enjoy opening portals, little treasure," Jagger teased.

Well now I didn't feel bad at all about his confusion. Nope, not in the least.

"And you can do way more than one cool thing," Breaker countered, offering me a winning smile that

I had to actively fight to not return. The way it made his eyes sparkle had my heart fluttering in a way that totally didn't help right now.

"Many cool things," Gage agreed, obviously trying to be supportive.

I responded only with a cool look, that what I really wanted to do was ask *'What cool things?'* I mean these guys were dragons, and while I was aware now that I was a dragon as well, I'd lived most of my life thinking I wasn't even a normal shifter, let alone a powerful one. So I was sort of curious what cool things they thought I could do...

Before I could ask, though, I became completely distracted by the clearing we'd just entered. *Stunning* wasn't a good enough word to describe the visual experience in front of me.

The crystal blue skies were clear with the exception of a few perfectly white puffy clouds, yet despite the perfect weather, the air carried a hint of rain. The wind was warm as it rustled through the trees on all sides of us, the tinkling of wind chimes echoing softly. I smiled as I stopped mid-stride and knelt down to run my fingers over the grass, the soft silky texture unlike anything I'd experienced before.

I didn't know how to explain it properly, but I could almost feel the magic from the territory reaching out to me. It wasn't the type of magic I was used to though. This was saturated on an entirely different level, and the only thing I'd experienced that was remotely similar was when I'd met Deva and her male witches.

Even then, though, there was a different under-tone to it.

"They arranged for a carriage," Gage said, his words drawing my gaze to the far corner where a path led out of the clearing. A light blue and green carriage sat right in the center of the pathway, nearly camouflaged by the small delicate yellow wildflowers painted across its surface, matching the landscape surrounding it. So much so that I hadn't noticed it at first.

"Nice of them," Breaker mused, sounding humored by the concept although I wasn't sure why.

"Are they friendly? At least with the clans?" I asked.

"Not friendly, per se, but amicable," Jagger allowed. "I would imagine that four Storm Dragon heirs coming into their territory without a lot of preparation or a set diplomatic reason, though, has probably caused confusion, so they're probably erring on the side of 'overly polite.'"

"I agree," Gage grunted. "I don't think this will

cascade into a larger problem overall, but you can never be sure with the fae."

"Especially because they're never fucking straightforward," Breaker growled.

"How far do we think the drive will be?" I asked, eager to find out what they were talking about. While I'd never met a fae—at least that I could remember—I was curious about their inability to lie and the resulting evasiveness. It didn't seem to be a quality that my mates liked, and considering how blunt I could be, it would probably be something I found frustrating as well.

"I'm not sure," Gage answered. "Depends on the route. We'll want to keep an eye out on the road since we don't know which part of the territory they'll be taking us through."

"I'll sit up front with Jagger." Breaker nodded towards the front row of seats on the carriage—the place that normally the driver would sit while directing the horses—as we rounded the vehicle.

But there wasn't a driver there, and there were no horses... There was nothing. Just two silver pieces of rope suspended in the air.

"Magic?" I whispered in awe.

"Magic," Gage grunted, opening the door to the carriage and lifting me up and into the vehicle. I looked around curiously, admiring the whimsical paintings on the ceiling depicting different naturescapes in soft pastels. The experience was enhanced by the faint scent of lavender that wafted from the gold seat cushions, two benches facing one another on either side.

It was completely possible that Jagger was right—I was loving Natura so far. It was so fairy-tale-like.

"Good to go?" Breaker asked, leaning in the doorway of the carriage. I nodded eagerly, a giggle escaping my lips as Gage pulled me onto his lap. Breaker chuckled and closed the door, and the carriage rocked as my other two mates hopped onto the driver's bench.

Moments later, the carriage took off.

A squeak of excitement left my lips as the carriage sped down the path towards our unknown destination, and I leaned forward to look out the window as we passed through the dense forest. The light breaking through the canopy in random spots, lighting up the normally shaded environment, made it almost appear to be glowing as the wind rustled loud enough that I cracked the window open, letting in the breeze.

"I love your smile, cupcake," Gage whispered against the shell of my ear, causing me to lean back into him fully, shifting in his lap to get comfortable.

"Don't move like that," Gage warned, a rumble

escaping his throat. My thighs pressed together, realizing just how hard he was. I couldn't deny that I loved how much I affected him, even in small moments like this.

"Move like what?" I shifted again, unable to help myself, my skin breaking into shivers at the deep, primal sound that left his throat. When he suddenly tugged me further back against him and slid one hand down to my hip to hold me in place, a small surprised sound left my lips.

"Like you want to be bent over," he said, his voice holding a threat that was anything but. In fact, I couldn't help but want exactly that. The beautiful view outside was completely forgotten as I tilted my head up, savoring how he held me captive against him, his other hand sliding up to wrap around my throat in a delicate but firm way.

"But maybe I do," I teased, looking at his lips as he dipped down to brush a teasing kiss across them. Before he could pull away, I nipped his bottom lip and his grip on my throat tightened, causing my center to tighten as well.

Gage grunted against my lips. "I think that you knowing how much you affect me is somehow more tortuous than when you didn't know."

"No, because now we can do something about it," I murmured hopefully. The rough hand on my hip slid down my leg to push up my dress, and the way his fingers trailed up my soft skin, caused me to nearly tremble with excitement.

"And what should we do, cupcake?" he demanded softly, but before I could answer, he nipped my ear and said, "Spread your legs."

I eagerly pushed further back against him and let my legs fall to either side of his massive frame, his cock wedged right against my butt and his finger trailing over my covered center. A shiver of need rolled over me as his lips brushed over his mating mark on my throat, Gage realizing how turned on I was from his mere teasing touch.

"Have you been needy all day, Bex? Is that why you wore this outfit? Hoping that one of us would push up your skirt and make you come?"

"Yes," I whimpered, loving that even a simple outfit could even affect my mates this much. I didn't think there was anything I could wear that they wouldn't want to rip off me, and that was so incredibly empowering.

"I can't fuck you," he growled. "Too many possible dangers on the road."

"Gage." I felt a small surge of panic that he would leave me in this state of need for him.

"But I won't leave you in pain," he promised as his fingers slid underneath my panties and rolled my wetness over my clit, causing me to arch, a moan leaving my throat and interrupting his hot words.

When his other hand left my throat and went to the laces on my corset, I watched as he untied it just enough that the straps fell at my shoulders and allowed him access to my skin. Without hesitation, he tugged down the material of the dress underneath and cupped my breast roughly, his fingers toying with my nipple. I tightened around his fingers as he slid two thick digits inside of me, nearly climaxing on the spot.

"Fuck, you are so tight," he groaned, sucking hard on my neck and causing my eyes to flutter shut, a dangerous inferno of need growing inside of me—one that demanded release.

"Gage, I need—"

"I know what you need, cupcake." He suddenly pulled his fingers from my center and licked them, making me moan at the sight alone. "But if you're going to come, it's going to be on my lips."

Suddenly, I was shifted onto the bench across from him, his massive frame spreading my legs as he tugged my panties to the side. His tongue running along my slit had me nearly detonating as my fingers tightened in his hair.

"You taste like fucking heaven," he groaned, then

pressed his tongue inside of me. My toes curled at the sensation, my moan filling the small vehicle.

Before I could beg him to make me come, Gage took mercy on me and sucked hard on my clit as he slid a finger back inside of me. Like a tsunami, I was hit hard with a euphoric pleasure that washed over me, drowning out everything else that wasn't Gage and me.

A buzzing sensation went over me, and every ounce of tension I'd been holding since last night began to fade away. My eyes were closed and I melted into the carriage bench, Gage murmuring something soft and sweet as he adjusted my panties and skirt before moving up to my corset.

I watched him with what I knew was a dreamy gaze as he adjusted and tied that as well before looking up at me—although even kneeling between my legs, he was larger than me.

"I think I love that look even more than your smile." He chuckled softly.

"I love you," I whispered, and his eyes filled with a wave of emotion that I knew he didn't really show outside of our small family.

"I love you more than I can ever express," he said seriously.

As he sat back on the bench, I crawled into his lap. Tucking myself against him, I continued to look outside the window with a relaxed interest—until we broke out of the forest.

Immediately I sat up, absolutely in awe.

While I hadn't seen a lot or traveled as much as others, I could easily say that Natura was the most beautiful territory in this realm.

Chapter 18

Gage Bronzeheart

The late afternoon light cast the capital city in a gold hue as our carriage barreled towards it. Bexley was curled against my chest as we passed through small village after small village, the houses an odd mix of medieval and modern. I was thankful to observe the latter, because that probably meant they had showers and other modern amenities. I hoped that was the case—I wasn't going to have my mate putting up with some medieval bullshit for long.

Although if it meant her wearing the type of dress she had on today, I wouldn't exactly complain. Not only did she look beautiful in it, but I could tell she loved it. In fact, Bexley seemed captivated by the view outside and the territory in general...I just hoped that this trip went as smoothly as we hoped.

So far, it was far better than Sanguis.

"I'm assuming that the Crown Prince will meet us on our arrival," I told her softly, smoothing a hand through her hair. "I would avoid talking to the fae if you can help it—I know it's not completely possible, but they aren't exactly safe."

I was also probably being grossly overprotective, but that wasn't going to stop anytime soon.

"Are they as dangerous as vampires?" Bexley frowned, worry filling her gaze. I knew it wasn't for herself, either—no, I had no doubt it was in reference to her mates.

"No," I assured her. "In fact, they aren't violent unless they need to be. Although they're more than capable—their magic is directly tied to nature and the land itself."

"So why are they dangerous?"

"Their magic can bind you to them if you say the wrong thing. Because of their inability to lie, they're evasive like we mentioned, but they also take the word of others very seriously. If you say something, they will take it at face value and hold you to it. And if you promise them anything, you're bound to them."

Bexley looked baffled. "That seems intense. I would hate to live like that, constantly having to watch what I am saying."

"I assume it's easier if you've lived in this society your entire life, but I've also heard that their magic goes a long way to guide them and tells them when to be careful."

"I may just try to stay quiet," Bexley said. "I sort of say exactly what I'm thinking and I don't want to mess anything up."

Cupping her jaw, I kissed her nose. "You never mess anything up, Bex. I didn't mean to scare you—worst case if you did get bound to someone through a promise, I would just kill them. Then you'd be free."

My mate's eyes widened almost comically. "Gage, you can't just—"

"Kill someone for trying to trap my mate into a magic promise? I sure can."

"Well, hopefully it won't come to that," she murmured, shaking her head and resting it back on my chest. I hoped that as well.

As we entered the capital city, a few people looked our way as they went about their evening activities, closing up market shops and walking home, but overall they didn't pay us much mind. Until we reached the castle gates—then I heard far more voices and commotion.

"Should we step out?" Bexley asked, hearing Breaker talking to the guards.

"No, they've got this," I promised her. And luckily, my word was supported when the gates opened only moments later with accompanying horns. Bex moved eagerly in her seat to look out the window with me as I took stock of the courtyard we were entering.

The castle was traditional in nature, made mostly of stone, but the gardens in the courtyard and the ivy climbing the walls softened the nature of the naturally intimidating dominance the building had over the kingdom. It was massive compared to every-thing else.

When the carriage stopped, I slid out the door, blocking Bex from doing the same until I could scope the area.

"It's all good, he's coming to meet us," Breaker said. Jagger offered me a nod from where he was talking to the captain of the guard near the front of the carriage. I could feel magic in the air, but everyone appeared to be relaxed, and more impor-tantly, unsurprised by our appearance. Which I suppose was good because sometimes people reacted poorly when surprised. Although our advanced notice also gave them an opportunity to plan shit.

"Gage," Bexley sang, and I smirked, stepping away from the door and letting her out of the carriage. I felt the guards' attention shift to her, and I had to control the rumble that broke from my chest. I hadn't been able to stop it from escaping, but I managed to tone it down just slightly. Luckily for them, it got the point across, and they immediately diverted their attention elsewhere.

Specifically onto the castle doors that opened to reveal a somewhat familiar face.

I'd only met him a handful of times, but I was glad that we were dealing with him rather than the Queen of the territory—a woman that, while he wouldn't admit to it, even managed to scare my dad a bit. I didn't want anything here to scare my mate.

Then again, my mom loved Queen Magnolia, so maybe Bexley would feel the same.

"Gage, Breaker, Jagger—good to see you three!" Prince Barrett greeted us, waving his soldiers out of the way in an attempt to remove a barrier from between all of us.

I couldn't deny the fae soldiers this—including the Crown Prince—while fae magic itself didn't come across as lethal on surface level alone, every single one of them appeared to be warriors in their own right. If I had to guess, that magic they had could instantly turn deadly if called upon.

"Thanks for the carriage," Breaker said. "We've been traveling a lot, and it was much easier than trying to find our way here on our own."

"Of course. I was surprised by your notice of

travel, but you're always welcome." Barrett came to a stop as his eyes landed on Bexley, only pausing for a moment before he looked at the three of us in surprise. "You've brought your mate."

Smart choice, diverting his gaze. Maybe fae weren't that different from us after all.

"Bexley," my cupcake offered with a smile. "Bexley Blackforge."

While I preferred my last name, I couldn't help but love how she stated hers so confidently.

His gaze darted to her in confusion before he looked back to Jagger, who explained, "It's a bit of a long story, but she's the lost heir of the clan that was killed in our territory around eight years ago."

"I see." Barrett nodded slowly, something like realization filling his gaze. "I have a feeling why you're here then."

I arched a brow as he turned to the guard and shouted something in an unfamiliar language, causing them to clear out immediately. When the castle door shut, the Prince motioned for us to follow him towards a group of benches in the garden nearby.

"This is beautiful," Bexley said softly.

"My mother takes a lot of pride in the castle gardens. She would love to hear that," Barrett replied, keeping his gaze ahead.

"Is your mom the Queen?" Bexley asked.

"She is—she's traveling in another section of the territory right now or else she would have loved to be here to greet the four of you."

As we all made ourselves comfortable on the benches, Barrett began to pace. "A year ago, we had a traveler arrive from Sanguis."

He'd already had our attention, but now we were riveted.

"We don't often accept visitors, especially from territories with rather violent reputations," he admitted unapologetically. "But this was no ordinary visitor, and her plea and explanation, while confusing at the time for both my mother and me, is making a lot more sense now."

"Was it Rebecca?" Bexley asked hopefully. "She has magic, but I believe she's part shifter as well."

"She didn't go by that name—in fact, she didn't give us a name." Barrett frowned. "But she explained that she was waiting for someone here—someone that would soon remember her. Someone that had survived the death of an entire dragon clan. We knew at that time she was talking about the Black-forge clan—everyone had heard the news—but I'm going to assume that she was talking about you. The heir to the Blackforge clan."

"If it's who I think it is, then yes, she was talking about me."

"We offered her sanctuary," Barrett said, finally sitting. "She's in one of the outer villages near the forest and farmlands where many of our gatherers live. It's about an hour or so from here. Not far."

"Let's go!" Bexley tried to pop up from the bench, but I pulled her back down.

"We'd like to see her as soon as possible," I said.

Barrett held my gaze for a long moment. "Of course. Let me prepare my carriage and I'll take us there tonight."

Well that had been far simpler than I'd expected.

"You're coming with us?" Jagger asked, and even I offered the Prince a look because that seemed more than a bit generous.

"Yes." He stood, his gaze conflicted, but I was almost positive it had nothing to do with us. "I've been needing to visit anyway. Give me half an hour. In the meantime, I'll have dinner brought to you."

Then the bastard was gone.

"Well he seems friendly," Bexley said happily.

"He is. He's actually the person I would rather deal with," Breaker admitted. "His mom would probably question our motives further."

"I wonder why he wants to come with," Jagger added.

"Probably a friend he wants to see," Bexley guessed. The castle doors opened and guards filled the edges of the space once more, along with attendants carrying a table and refreshments. At least we didn't have to go inside.

I didn't like the idea of being inside a castle that was unfamiliar to me. Being out here in the open air made me much more comfortable since I'd be able to get Bex out of here immediately if needed. I had a feeling that Barrett understood that and that's why he hadn't pushed for us to follow him inside.

"I'm not sure the Crown Prince would have many friends out in the villages," I said. Bexley's nose scrunched in confusion, making me nearly chuckle. Yeah, I knew my mate wouldn't understand that logic—after all, this woman was a storm dragon who was best friends with a bunny. Bexley didn't give a shit about societal status, and it was one of many things I loved about her.

"Oh, food!" Bexley clapped happily as the scent of steak filled the air. My chest relaxed slightly as I kissed the side of her head, encouraging her to eat.

I'd take my wins where I could, because I had a feeling it was going to be a long night, whether or not we found Rebecca.

* * *

The carriage ride felt far shorter than an hour. I sat in the front next to Barrett, talking occasionally about the passing landscape and updating him on our own territory. In return he explained some of the politics going on in his territory, but on the whole he was far quieter than he'd been at the castle. The silence wasn't uncomfortable, but it wasn't the only thing that had changed about him.

Rather than using the fancy carriage we'd arrived in, he'd chosen a more 'normal' one, less decorated and with actual horses leading the way. He'd also chosen to forgo wearing a crown or anything that would symbolize his position of power.

He didn't explain or comment on it, and I finally decided to ask as the carriage began to slow. Lights began to dot the landscape in the distance, and a village cast in the twilight light from above appeared out of seemingly nowhere.

"No crown?"

Barrett tensed, then sighed. "The person I need to talk to...she doesn't realize who I am. It's never been the right time to tell her."

Bexley hadn't been wrong, it was a friend—but I had a feeling it was far more than that.

"She wouldn't like that you're the Prince?"

Barrett's voice took on a defensive tone. "It's not

that she wouldn't like it, I just think the attention from the position would..."

"Be something she hates?" I suggested.

"Yeah," Barrett grunted. I nodded as if I understood, although I didn't fully get the problem. But before I could attempt to offer any advice, we were pulling through the village on the main road.

People emerged from their houses to see what was going on, and some walked alongside the carriage as we traveled towards town square. Lights floated in the air all around it, and it was filled with people dancing to music. Bexley was going to love this.

"Not the best timing," Barrett muttered. "I didn't realize they were having a festival."

"Allows us a bit more privacy?" I offered. His eyes scanned the area, and he pulled the carriage to a stop when he found whatever it was he'd been looking for. I followed his line of sight, but before I could ask what the hell he was doing, the bastard was out of the carriage and striding towards the festivities.

"What's going on?" Bexley asked, climbing to sit on the bench next to me.

I nodded toward the dance floor, where Barrett had interrupted a couple dancing. "*That* is why

Barrett wanted to come with us," I said, a big smile on my face.

Chapter 19

Bexley Blackforge

The village we stopped in could only be described as ethereal. Sitting next to Gage at the front of the carriage, I was able to take in so much at once—from the quaint houses on either side of the roads, some of them featuring market-like stands, to the town square that was decorated in fairy lights that danced in the twilight sky. Classical music filled the air along with laughter and the scent of food, creating a cocoon of what could almost be called 'love' that emanated from the villagers.

They were the reason this place was filled with a visceral warmth and happiness.

I swayed with the music as I noticed small little details of the natural magic that was innate to the fae. Flowers along the edge of the dance floor went through the cycle of blossoming and closing back up in conjunction with the music, and the wind itself acted as a dance partner to those twirling on their own in the center of the gathering space.

There was only one thing—and three people—that seemed to be drawing away from the happiness. I only knew one of them: Prince Barrett.

Despite being one of the only fae I'd met—well, really the only one since I suppose just seeing his guards didn't count as meeting them—his presence was impactful and had set the tone for my impression thus far. Not only was he extremely powerful, but he came across as earnest and honest. It may have been total bullcrap, but I didn't think so.

He was also huge. I wasn't sure why—maybe because of storybook fairy tales—but in my head I'd had this vision of fae being delicate and dainty. All the men I'd seen so far were anything but, including Barrett. Something that was only highlighted by the woman he was standing next to.

She stared up at him with confusion and naturally leaned away from the man she'd been dancing with, who was shorter and far less intimidating than Barrett, his face turning red in anger. For just a moment, the woman's gaze met my own before moving away, but it was enough to spur me into climbing down from the carriage and walking towards them.

"Bexley!" Breaker shouted, but I weaved between the partygoers until I was standing right in front of the woman. She had to be right around my age, and we were nearly the same build and size, except she was slightly shorter than me. She was also stunning.

All the women in my life were beautiful in their own right, but I had to admit that she was more unique. Her hair was dark at the roots, turning silver until just past her shoulders where it turned into a spring green that matched her grass-colored gaze. A gaze that was filled with concern as she looked at me for a long moment before returning her attention to Barrett, moving slightly closer to him.

That was when I tuned into the conversation.

"You shouldn't even be here, Barrett," the other man spit out. "You should be back in the capital. And you even brought strangers with you this time."

"You live in the capital?" the woman asked, her brow dipping in confusion.

Barrett tensed even more but wrapped a soothing arm around her. "Yes," he said softly, fixing the man with a stern look as he added, "And who I bring here is none of your damn business."

"Strangers, that would be us," I interrupted,

trying to defuse the situation but keeping my gaze on her. "My mates and I came here looking for someone. We're not trying to cause problems."

"Oh." The woman offered a small smile after looking towards my mates, seeming to relax slightly. "Well, if you're friends of Barrett then you're welcome here."

"Hazel—"

"We can talk later," she assured the other man, though she didn't hold his gaze. Then, leaving both the men behind, she motioned for me to follow her out of the crowded space. I heard Barrett say something in a threatening tone, but I couldn't hear exactly what.

"Thank you for coming over; that could have gone badly," she said softly before offering me a tiny smile. "Burke is someone I've been in school with for a long time, and recently he's been kind of pushy."

"That's not good." I frowned. "Pushy about what?"

Her gaze darkened as we finally broke free of the crowd, but she didn't lower her voice accordingly, so it was very clear when she said, "About marrying me."

Before I could say a word, Barrett was in front of her looking pissed. Enough so that she leaned back, prompting me to gently squeeze her arm in silent support. I barely knew this woman, but I felt a kinship to her that I couldn't fully explain.

"What did you say?" Barrett asked, fully focused on her as if nothing else but what she had to say mattered.

"He wants me to marry him. Has for a while." She shrugged, clearly trying to not make it a big deal. "I've told him no, but I'm running out of excuses. After all, I'm pretty much stuck in this town, so what else is there to do?"

"So many fucking things. You are not marrying him," Barrett gritted out. Then he walked back towards the carriage without another word, likely to try and calm down. My mates moved to talk to him, and the woman next to me watched with interest and a bit of sadness.

"Hazel, right?" I asked, remembering the name the man had called her.

"Yes." She nodded, her gaze moving to mine.

"I'm Bexley," I offered cheerfully. "And I don't know who that other jerk Burke is, but you don't have to marry him."

"I don't," she agreed, looking around the village center. "But it's what everyone else does. I mean, it'll happen eventually. It's not like I'm going to be whisked away somewhere else. My family has lived here for generations."

But from the way she looked at Barrett, I had a feeling that was exactly what she wanted.

"Maybe that will happen," I suggested. "Barrett doesn't want you to marry him."

"Barrett doesn't know what he wants. He disappears for days and comes to visit maybe once a week but never tells me why. I didn't even know he lived in the capital!" she exclaimed, rolling her eyes. "He could be the freakin' King of the territory for all I know."

Wait...did she not know? Oh my fates, *she didn't know.*

"He must be coming here for a reason," I said, knowing it wasn't my place to fix this...but at the same time, I could see how much all of this was affecting her.

"Plus, I don't want my escape from this town to be because of a guy," she mumbled more to herself than to me.

That was when an idea popped into my head.

"What about DIA, Dark Imaginarium Academy? We have to be around the same age, right? I just started there and I think you would love it!"

Hazel laughed, her eyes shining with authentic amusement. "I could never get in there—no one does unless they have money or influence. I think the people in my class will take the test this upcoming spring, and I haven't even been given information on it let alone actually considered going...there just wouldn't be a point."

So she was a year younger than me? Good to know.

"You should take the test," Barrett said, returning to the conversation and bringing my mates with him. "You should take it, Hazel. Trust me. I'll be taking it as well."

"You think so?" She asked, her eyes filled with a small amount of hope. "Maybe. I mean, if you're going to take it too, I wouldn't feel as weird about it. Although the chances of me getting in, let alone being able to afford it—"

"Hey." I squeezed her arm again. "I promise, if you want to go to DIA, we'll make it happen."

The word 'promise' had a squeak leaving her lips as magic sparked in the air. Gage muttered a curse, Jagger looked concerned, and Breaker appeared surprised but more amused than anything at the sudden influx of power.

"What just happened?"

"You made a promise, a pact with me." Hazel's eyes shone with emotion. "Why would you do that?"

"Oh." I shrugged. "I mean, I can tell how much you want to get out of this village, and I really do think you would like DIA, so I'm serious—if you want to go, we will make it happen."

This time it was my turn to let out a surprised noise as Hazel tugged me into a hug that was so tight I nearly winced. I couldn't tell how Barrett felt about the situation—he didn't look unhappy, though. Almost shocked and maybe resigned—although to what I wasn't sure.

"Right." He motioned towards the road on the other side of the square. "Now that we have that handled, do you want to come with us to show them where Rebecca lives?"

Hazel pulled back from the hug, offering me another smile before she processed his words. "Rebecca? Absolutely. Although it may be a bit late for her."

"She'll want to see us," Jagger promised. Hazel let out a satisfied sound and then turned back towards the festival, beginning to make her way through the crowd. Leaving our carriage behind, we followed, Barrett jogging ahead of her as my mates pulled me close. I gave them all a hopeful look as we continued forward, and when we broke from the crowd I noticed that Barrett had his arm around Hazel again and they were talking in quiet tones.

"That was nice of you," Breaker murmured.

I shrugged. "I meant it."

Gage kissed the side of my head, seemingly more relaxed about the situation that I would have assumed considering the warning he'd given me. Maybe he thought I didn't know what I was doing, but I didn't make promises lightly. This one just happened to tie me with magic to a girl who I felt like was meant to be my friend.

"I think she would've ended up leaving here either way, but you sure made his job easier," Jagger said. "Now he doesn't have to convince her to go."

"I didn't realize that she doesn't know..." I drew out, not wanting to say it aloud.

"I still don't get that," Gage agreed.

Any further conversation on the topic was put on hold as it became quiet enough that my attention was drawn to an approaching cabin. It was smaller than the others in the village and covered in ivy. Smoke poured from the chimney and the windows were covered in drapes, but it didn't stop the scent of herbs from drifting through.

A shadow passed across the drapes, and a nervous excitement invaded my chest. When the door creaked open, I came to a stop as a dark cloaked figure stepped out of the cozy home. I briefly noticed that Barrett and Hazel had stepped back slightly, fading into the shadows, but I could only focus on *her*.

Rebecca looked up, and her hood slid back, revealing her familiar scaled face and dark hair that was braided down one side of her head, resting on her shoulder. But the thing that stood out to me the most? The tears that were crowding her gaze.

"Bexley Blackforge, I've been waiting a long time for you."

Chapter 20

Bexley Blackforge

The hug that Rebecca engulfed me in instantly had tears filling my eyes as my arms tightened around the woman, feeling a wave of emotion that I didn't expect and didn't know how to deal with. Instead, I just embraced the emotion and let the tears stream down my cheeks, squeezing my eyes shut and taking in the moment.

"I am so glad you're here, sweet girl. That night..." She stuttered to a stop and pulled back, giving me a smile that didn't remove the sadness in her gaze. "We can talk about that soon. I'm just so glad you're here. I'm so glad that my clues weren't left in vain."

"They weren't," I promised. "I'm sorry I didn't come sooner. I didn't get my memories back until—"

"You turned eighteen and shifted," she finished

253

for me. "I know. I felt it." Her gaze moved over my shoulder. "And these are your mates. Boys, you never met me officially, but it's good to see all of you again."

Their small smiles and nods had Rebecca relaxing as she finally looked at Barrett and Hazel.

"I hope you two don't mind, but the five of us need to talk in private," she told them.

"We'll wait for you back at the festival in town," Hazel promised.

"Good, good," Rebecca said, inviting us to follow her inside her cottage.

When I stepped inside, I was engulfed in the world's sweetest scent. Each wall of the living area was decorated with shelves holding an assortment of bottles containing crystals, herbs, and various small objects. Above, hanging from the ceiling, were dried herbs, hanging plants, and stained glass that glinted in the candlelight and the roaring flames of the fireplace. I could see several doors leading from the room, but Rebecca motioned for us to sit on the comfortable couches gathered around the fireplace.

"Let me put on some tea and then we'll talk," she suggested. As she went into the kitchen, I used my hand to push away the tears on my cheek. Jagger pulled me onto his lap as Gage sat to our right, and Breaker took an armchair that was closer to the door, avoiding the loveseat that already held a cup of tea and blanket, most likely our host's.

"You okay, *mo chuisle?*" Breaker asked, his voice soft and serious.

"Yes, just a bit overwhelmed," I admitted.

Before my mates could ask me anything further, Rebecca returned with a tea kettle that she placed on an iron shelf over the fireplace. "Truthfully, I didn't know how long it would take for you to put all of this together and find me. I knew when the memory spell broke, but I couldn't tell anything past that. What led you to go back to your family's land?"

"I want to know what happened that night; what happened to my family," I whispered, my throat feeling tight. "What happened to my clan."

Rebecca nodded and knitted her fingers together. "Of course. I have to admit, I'm glad it was that and not something more troubling..."

I had a feeling she was talking about anything regarding Clanguard, but I didn't want to let her in on my assumptions just yet.

"What happened that night?" I prompted her, trying to keep my voice gentle. It didn't help that I was nearly unable to contain the impatience I felt. After traveling so many places over the course of just a few days, I needed to know what was going on. I needed the truth.

"That night was a result of something that happened long before, when you were younger than you probably remember," Rebecca said, her gaze going distant as she stared into the roaring fire.

"The Flash Clan was known for using prophetesses, which your mother hand selected, along with others in positions like myself. Where I was classified as a healer because of my unblessed witch magic, the prophetesses were descendants from the demigods and had the unique ability to glimpse into the future. They were accurate enough that your mother trusted them, but their visions were never extremely specific. That was, until the prophecy was given."

I swallowed, feeling a nervous tightness in my chest. "We recently discovered the prophecy as well. We began to search for it after I had a dream about it, and we found a book my mom kept of all prophecies given, big or small. She'd given it to Breaker's mom, who thought it was an accident, but now we think—"

"It wasn't an accident," Rebecca confirmed with a sentimental smile. "Your mom never did anything by accident. Everything was extremely well planned, especially when it came to you and your safety."

I nodded, once again trying to keep my emotions at bay.

"If I remember correctly, the prophecy was *'When the time comes that four lines are united by one heir who threatens everything created in the darkness, the territory will be made anew, reborn in the ashes of the cursed pack.'"*

"That's what the book said," Gage rumbled.

"As you can imagine, it was the type of prophecy that in the wrong hands could be dangerous. Your parents kept it a secret for quite a while, not even allowing it to be recorded right away. But it didn't matter because the prophecy was leaked by the prophetess, who told one of the only 'packs' it could apply to."

"Clanguard." Breaker's voice was hard, and all of us tensed because even hearing his name made me angry.

Rebecca examined all of our faces as her own anger surfaced and her jaw tightened. "It's as I feared, then? He's become a problem once more now that he knows you're alive?"

"Yes, he's attempted to turn other territory leaders against us by claiming we're planning to take over the city with our newly formed mating bond."

"He doesn't care about that, not truly." Rebecca's eyes darkened. "Clanguard had many reasons to want to attack your family, Bexley. From them helping his wife escape from his abusive hand to trying to stop the gross mistreatment of women that occurred under his reign...all of it would have been reason enough. But the prophecy was the tipping point, and not because he was worried about the four of you using your newly found bond to strive for more power. It wasn't fear that drove him to attack."

So we'd been right. He had been the one to attack that night—holy crap. Why did I feel like this wasn't the worst of it, though?

"What was it?" My stomach churned.

"Opportunity," Rebecca spit out. "Opportunity, Bexley. Linan is always striving for power, always striving for more—I would bet the plan was in place from the time you were revealed to be a storm dragon."

Oh no.

Jagger's hand tightened on me.

"The reason he attacked that night," Rebecca growled, "was in order to capture you, Bexley. Only you. He didn't care about anything else. Clanguard wanted you mated to his son so that you'd produce storm dragons that would be under his control."

My ears went static as I curled further into Jagger, whose chest was vibrating with a deep, dangerous noise. Gage was pacing now, unable to help the ferocious energy surrounding him, and Breaker was white-knuckling the chair.

"How do you know that?" I whispered.

"We learned that he planned to attack a week or

so before it occurred, but his true motive wasn't revealed until the day of. It was only by chance that our spy within his pack caught wind of the information, a faint whisper that clearly was grounded in truth. But even if our spy hadn't passed on that information, your parents weren't willing to risk it. They were going to send you off with me, and we were going to gather the other clans together, reveal what was happening—"

"Why didn't they tell the other clans before?" Gage demanded in a hard whisper.

"Because they didn't know who they could trust. At the time, Clanguard had spies everywhere, but he wasn't enough of a threat for the clans to exile them from their territories."

"So why the memory spell?"

"I was with your mom when the attack started, and when we saw Clanguard's forces... Well, we realized that the chances of me escaping with you to the neighboring clan lands were limited. It wasn't like we could just walk out the door. So I still planned on leaving with you, but I suggested a memory spell as well so that if anything did go wrong, you would at least be able to hide behind the fact that you had no memory of what you were."

I looked down at the fire as the teapot began to boil and ran a hand over my face, trying to collect my thoughts. But one thought rang loud and clear above all the others.

"So the entire clan and my parents died... because of me. Because Clanguard wanted to take me to be his son's—"

I couldn't even finish the sentence because Jagger's grip on me turned dangerously tight. Right now, though, it was one of the only things grounding me.

Rebecca's eyes darkened. "Your clan willingly died protecting you. Your clan, every single shifter in it, would have given their life ten times over for you."

"I don't care," I said harshly.

"Clanguard did take something that night, though." Rebecca stood, walking over to sit next to Jagger and me. My heart stuttered, really hoping that this wasn't going to make all of this so much worse.

"Something or someone?" I whispered.

"Two someones." Rebecca's eyes lit with furious anger. "Clanguard took your parents captive—both of them."

"What?" All four of us froze, shock permeating through our bond.

"Your parents aren't dead, Bexley. Clanguard has them."

* * *

Alive. My parents were alive...

We were still silent as Rebecca began to pour tea, and tears spilled freely down my cheeks. How was she thinking about tea right now? My parents were alive, and she was pouring tea... That just didn't make sense in my head. I covered my mouth as a sob threatened to leave my lips.

"How do you know after all this time..." Breaker's voice was filled with pain as he leaned forward and gently squeezed my hand in support.

"I don't have confirmation—not true confirmation," Rebecca allowed before pressing a hand to the center of her chest, right over her heart. "But I *know*. I can feel it. Your parents' magical signatures were extremely strong, and I was around them enough that I became attuned to it. They're still alive. I don't know where, and I have no idea how Clanguard is managing to keep them imprisoned—"

"For eight fucking years," Jagger cursed.

"But they're alive; I would bet everything on it." Rebecca placed cups of tea in front of us, and I stared at mine before taking a small sip. The burning hot water didn't even faze me as I continued to stare at her.

"Why wouldn't you tell someone before now?" I asked.

Rebecca froze and held my gaze. "I made a vow

to your mother, and more importantly, you, that was tied to your own memory spell. I vowed that I would not reveal the details of what happened to anyone but you since we didn't know who we could trust. I couldn't tell you until your memory spell broke, and by then I was here and I figured you would find me. If I'd tried to say anything, it would have caused the same level of pain that trying to remember your past caused you."

"It would also ensure that if you were captured you wouldn't say anything," Breaker murmured.

"Torture is a breaker of vows," Rebecca mused. "I trust myself, but I didn't want to leave any room for error. So no, I wasn't able to say anything about your parents—but now I have."

"I have no idea how it's possible that he would be able to keep two adult dragons—one storm and the other—"

"Fire. Bexley's mother's power was fire focused," she answered Gage as he continued to pace.

Standing up and taking a long sip of tea before placing it down, I nibbled my lip. "We have to find them. We have to break them out. I don't care what it takes."

"Do not rush into this," Rebecca begged me quietly. "Clanguard may seem like just a normal wolf shifter, even if powerful, but the man is involved in some very dangerous things. Do not underestimate him, Bexley."

I believed her. I mean, the man had the confidence and ability to take on an entire Storm Dragon Clan and defeat them successfully. That was terrifying.

"Now I understand why these past few years he's grown more paranoid about his pack's territory and vetting every single shifter who wants to join—it's become more oppressive than ever, almost militaristic," Breaker said. "I figured it was why his pack members were lashing out and committing crimes through the rest of the city but now it feels like more of a cover to hide something larger."

"We need to tell our parents," Jagger said quietly. "The other clan leaders need to be informed of what's going on now that we have absolute confirmation. This isn't a decision we can move forward on without everyone being on the same page."

I nodded and sat back down in a trance, only half listening to the conversation. Only one thought kept looping through my mind—*My parents are alive*. My mom and dad...were alive.

But what if Rebecca was wrong? What if she'd mistaken... No, I had to believe her. I had to keep that small smidge of hope from being extinguished—

that just maybe my mom and dad were alive, simply waiting for a rescue.

I wasn't entirely positive how long the five of us sat there in quiet conversation as Rebecca continued to tell us, mostly my mates, any other small details she could recall from that night. She described the type of military force they'd used, especially while unshifted, and small snippets of things that were yelled in the midst of battle. Eventually, once I'd finished two cups of tea and the fire began to burn itself out, my emotions were steadying themselves.

There was still a shakiness to my frame, and when I put the mug down my fingers trembled. But the fire was keeping me warm, and having my mates so nearby helped regulate my rapid heartbeat. I felt more determined than ever to stop Clanguard, and while I felt off and more than a bit emotional, it didn't change what we had to do.

Linan Clanguard would pay for what he did to my clan, and he would doubly pay for what he'd done to my parents—because I knew that if they were alive, the last eight years had been...horrible. That didn't even seem like a good enough word to describe it though. I couldn't even imagine what they'd endured. It made my stomach queasy to even consider.

"Will you be coming back with us?" I asked

Rebecca as they began discussing the need to go back to our territory and tell the others. If she was surprised by my question, she didn't reveal it and instead offered me a small smile.

"I will follow. My magic has grown tired over the years, but I will help in any way that I can now that I'm free to speak on what happened," she said. "I'll need a few days, though, to gather what I need before following behind."

"We'll send for someone to wait by the portal and take you to the Silvershade estate," Jagger said. "It's where we're going to go once we get back."

It was a good idea. Not only was I eager to see his home and where he'd grown up, but it wasn't the time to go back to DIA. Now more so than ever.

"Then that's what we will do." Rebecca stood, motioning for me to join her. I melted into her hug as she gave me another, and the maternal, almost grand-motherly warmth that came off of her soothed a small part of my soul.

I had to keep it together. I didn't want to cry anymore.

I wasn't usually one to stop myself from it, but I was absolutely exhausted from the emotions roaring through me, and at this point I was physically exhausted as well.

"If you're going to get on the road, I would

suggest taking one of Barrett's spelled carriages," she said, pulling back and walking slowly towards the door. "The woods can be dangerous at night."

"Hopefully they're still waiting for us." I looked down the path outside of her home, noticing glowing lights in the distance from the village.

"Oh, they will be. If Hazel is up, then Barrett is there," Rebecca mused. "Sweet girl, but she needs to get out of this village."

"I promised I would get her into the academy we attend."

"You made a promise to a fae." Rebecca shook her head in amusement. "Well, if there was any fae to trust with a promise, it's her. And I know that you would never promise something you don't intend to do, Bexley —you've been like that since you were very young."

Offering a small smile at her wistful tone, I squeezed her hand. "I'll see you soon?"

"Few days behind at most," she promised and then looked at my mates. "Get her home safe, boys."

"Always," Gage rumbled, kissing the top of my head.

When Rebecca shut her door and we made our way down the shadowed path, a sense of determination rolled over me, overpowering any sadness. I knew my mates could feel the change as well because we walked in comfortable silence, their low, deep voices only interrupting it to discuss logistics on getting back and to the Silvershade estate. It wasn't until we reached the town square that we ran into anyone else.

And even then it was just Hazel and Barrett. The two of them were sitting underneath the fairy lights and laughing about something, making me smile. It was so incredibly obvious how much the two of them cared for one another...but then again, maybe it wasn't obvious to Hazel. I could hardly blame her; I'd been in a similar position myself with Gage for most of the past eight years.

"Oh, you're done!" Hazel hopped up. "I'm so glad we waited."

"We do need to get to the portal though," Breaker said to Barrett.

"We can take you—right, Barrett?"

Barrett nodded and indicated the carriage waiting for us, the horses waiting nearby at a water trough.

"Awesome." Hazel tugged my hand, and I smiled as I followed along. "Now you can tell me everything I need to know on the way there."

"About?" I asked, already feeling a bit more light around my friend.

"Dark Imaginarium Academy. I want to know everything."

Chapter 21

Bexley Blackforge

The familiar scent of my mates surrounded me as warmth cocooned me, the soft material of the velvet comforter beneath my cheek making me sigh happily. Before even opening my eyes, I racked my brain for where I was, exactly, and what I remembered last...but found myself drawing a blank. Continuing to let myself float in a relaxed state of sleepiness, I took stock of what I could feel around me.

I was alone and stretched out on a comfortable bed. I also recognized that I was somewhere safe... Memories began to seep in, and I let my eyes open to confirm what I already knew.

I was at the Silvershade estate.

Last night had been such a whirlwind between everything I'd learned and the questions Hazel had for me about DIA. I must have fallen asleep just after we traveled through the portal. I remembered saying goodbye to her and Barrett and then getting into the car that was waiting for us, but everything else was fuzzy. I didn't even remember getting to the Silvershade estate, at least visually; only the soft murmurs of my mates' and his parents' distant voices had alerted me that we'd reached our destination.

As I blinked, the afternoon sun hitting me right in the face, I felt a further tug of confusion because... how freakin' long had I been sleeping? It must have been a good amount of time because it was not only Monday, but Monday afternoon—*well* into the day.

It couldn't have been longer than that, right? There was no way.

Sitting up and looking around, I took a moment to appreciate Jagger's bedroom. The massive bed was covered in a velvet silver comforter that matched the chrome accents throughout the room. Everything else was an onyx color that should have left the space feeling cold, but paired with the warm afternoon sunlight and the fireplace, which was crackling, the room had a cozy ambiance.

I absolutely loved it...but where were my mates? I listened quietly for a moment before determining they weren't here and I was probably going to have to go looking for them.

Letting out a groan and stretching my arms above my head, I slipped out of bed and walked beneath the black marble archway that led to the bathroom suite. The minute I stepped in, lights flooded the room, and a pleased noise left my throat at the massive tub in the center of the space. It was raised with a curved lip on all sides except where the steps were to get into it. The floors slanted around it and led to what was probably a hidden drain, making me wonder if it was meant to recycle the water over and over again.

If that was the case, I was absolutely taking a long soak in the tub.

I knew my mates would come back eventually, and while I wouldn't have minded exploring the estate, my brain was fuzzy and I felt drained from everything that had occurred lately. A little alone time was exactly what I needed.

As the tub filled up, I added some lavender scented soap and pulled off my dress, my corset and boots long gone. Letting out another yawn, I stepped into the hot water and groaned, sinking all the way down until just my head was at the surface. A shiver of happiness rolled over me, and I positioned myself in the far corner before closing my eyes, allowing the water to soothe my skin.

I couldn't tell how long I was in the tub exactly,

but between scrubbing my hair and body, then relaxing a bit more, it felt like it had been at least an hour. When my stomach started rumbling, though, I knew it was time to get out. There was one thing that could overshadow relaxing every time, and it was being hungry.

Wrapping myself in a robe, I walked towards the vanity and found my cosmetic bag set out, so I quickly brushed my teeth before blow drying my hair and applying some light makeup. I didn't know what the day would hold for us, but the calming, familiar routine had me feeling far better as I walked back into the bedroom.

Hearing movement from the other room and figuring it wasn't my mates since they hadn't just walked into the bedroom, I quickly got dressed, deciding to wear a pair of high-waisted loose jeans and a soft golden off-the-shoulder sweater. It was comfortable, and paired with socks and some slides, I felt remarkably better than I had before.

Now I just needed iced coffee and a cupcake. And maybe some real food...but that didn't sound nearly as appealing.

"Bexley, I'm so glad you're awake," Mrs. Silver-shade said as I stepped into the attached living suite, finding her sitting on the couch and flipping through some books. "I was getting worried, especially with how exhausted you were last night."

Her concern warmed my chest. "Sorry about that. I remember coming here...briefly, but after everything else last night I was so incredibly tired."

"I can imagine," she said, sliding me a cup of tea after pouring water from a teapot. "Traveling into a new territory is one thing, but two in one weekend? That would render even the strongest of us exhausted."

Before I could agree, she offered me a knowing smile. "Although I think you may qualify as the 'strongest of us.' I heard you can open a portal on your own."

A bit of pride surged through me. "I was surprised by that too. Honestly, I've been surprised by a lot this past weekend."

Her eyes darkened with a mixture of sadness and anger that I had a feeling she was trying to keep controlled. "Jagger told us everything. If it wasn't Rebecca telling you all of this, I'd find it hard to believe. Especially the prospect of them being alive."

I could hear the hope in her voice, and I clung to it. "You know Rebecca?"

"Oh yes. She didn't go out in public or make herself available often, but she was your mother's closest advisor, always by her side in private."

Which probably explained the closeness I felt towards her. While I didn't have many specific memories I could recall with her in them, I had a feeling she'd always been there.

I wanted to ask more, but of course right at that moment my stomach growled.

"You're hungry," Mrs. Silvershade said in realization, my cheeks heating. "Of course you are; you've slept over twelve hours. And here I am having tea with you. Follow me, we'll go straight to the kitchen."

"Thanks," I said as we left the bedroom suite and made our way down a long hallway, the motif of metallic shades and contrasting stone seeming to echo through the rather modern estate. I wasn't sure what I'd expected from the Silvershade estate, but this was far more grand than even the Bronzeheart estate...and that was saying something.

Finally breaking the comfortable silence between us, I asked, "Twelve hours? It's Monday afternoon?"

She nodded as we made our way across a grand foyer with a winding staircase and full glass window walls. "I was going to wake you up soon—the boys have been running around making plans—but I couldn't bring myself to actually do it, so instead I got tea."

"Thanks for letting me get some rest," I said as

we turned the corner into an all white marble kitchen, the sunlight shining through the window making it sparkle like it was embedded with diamonds. "Your house is absolutely beautiful, by the way."

"Thank you," said, leading me to a seat at the kitchen island. "It's taken years to get it exactly how I want it, but it's finally there. I don't think my son likes it all that much, but I can never really tell."

I tilted my head curiously at that as she took out some leftovers and began to put them onto a plate to heat up. Hadn't Jagger said something similar about his parents, about how they didn't express their emotions well? Or were reserved? I thought Jagger and his mom were very expressive, but maybe I was seeing a different side of them.

Then again, everyone was far more comfortable in their own homes.

"I'm not a great cook, but these are leftovers from dinner. If you want something more breakfast oriented, I can call the chef—"

"This is perfect," I promised as she put the plate in front of me, fresh out of the microwave. When a deep voice sounded in the hallway, I instantly perked up, keeping my gaze on the kitchen archway as Jagger made his way through.

"Mom, have you seen—"

"Morning!" I chimed. Jagger's gaze went from his mom, who was making coffee and seemingly enjoying keeping herself busy, to me at the island. Relief instantly filled my mate's face as he walked over, tilted my chin up, and kissed me hard enough that my food was long forgotten.

"See? She didn't go far." His mom's voice was like ice water. My cheeks turned bright red, and I pulled away, going back to eating my food and trying to pretend like I hadn't just been making out with her son a few feet away from her.

"Here, let me make that for her." Jagger rounded the island and took the coffee from his mom, then went to the freezer to grab a clear glass. I smiled happily as he turned the hot coffee into an iced one, and when I looked over at his mom, she was staring at him in surprise.

"Well, this is interesting to watch," she said, joining me at the kitchen island. When Jagger handed me the iced coffee and I gave him a quick kiss of thanks, he finally turned to his mom.

"What's interesting?"

"Oh, nothing," she mused, humming under her breath.

Jagger arched a brow but then returned his attention to me. "I'm glad you're eating. When you're done here we can go outside—Gage and Breaker are out on the patio with our guests."

"Guests?" I asked, wondering what had gone on while I was sleeping. His mom had mentioned them 'handling stuff,' but I hadn't thought to question it at the time.

"Yes, and they're only the first to arrive," he said.

"The clans and territory leaders are all coming here tonight to discuss what you've learned," his mom explained.

My chest tightened with anxiety. "I'm going to have to tell them everything Rebecca said?"

"Or we can," Jagger offered.

"I still feel so guilty," I said, unable to look at either of them. "I know no one will admit to blaming me, but Clanguard attacked because—"

"He's a bastard. He attacked because he's a bastard." Mrs. Silvershade's voice was hard, and I lifted my eyes to meet hers. "No other reason, Bexley. Do not blame yourself for a grown man's decision. He targeted a child. He wanted to kidnap you. He is at fault here, absolutely no one else."

Jagger kissed the top of my head as I inhaled, trying to take her words to heart. They did help the guilt to an extent, but of course they didn't completely remove it.

"I want to be the one to tell them tonight," I said.

"Since Rebecca won't be here for another couple days to tell them herself, it should be me."

"Whatever you want," Jagger agreed.

Nodding, I continued to eat a few more bites and finished my iced coffee, a question occurring to me as my brain fully woke up. "Wait, who arrived early?"

Jagger's eyes warmed. "Your bunny shifter friend —Rachel."

Except it wasn't just Rachel—it was Fletcher and Thomas Clanguard as well. To say I was shocked was the understatement of the century.

"Rachel!" My voice was a squeak as we stepped onto the patio, which overlooked a series of gardens with modern sculptural water features, the glint of the water in the afternoon sun sparkling like gemstones.

Rachel immediately turned, rushing out of her seat to give me a hug. "I'm so glad you're awake! I was worried when they mentioned how long you'd been sleeping."

"I can't believe you're here." I pulled back, immensely happy to have such a good surprise after the series of unpleasant and confusing ones.

"We had to talk, and more importantly, Fletcher

had to explain," she said softly as I realized Jagger had made his way back to the table, allowing us a moment.

"Explain?" I asked cautiously.

"Come over, I promise it'll make sense." She squeezed my hand. "They were just telling us everything you learned—"

"Everything?" My brows shot up for several reasons. First because I didn't know what had changed to make my mates trust Fletcher. Secondly because the nature of what we'd discovered about the reason for the attack—Linan's plan to mate me to his son—was more than a bit uncomfortable, but especially in the face of Rachel being his mate.

"Yes, Linan's an absolute—" Rachel took a deep breath as if stopping herself from saying something harsher. Once she'd gathered herself, she finished with, "He's a piece of crap."

That was putting it mildly, but I understood her point.

"Cupcake." Gage tugged me gently onto the chair between himself and Breaker, the latter giving me a kiss on the top of my head. Jagger stood behind me, and I couldn't deny I felt centered, between them as I was.

"Morning," I told them softly, even though for everyone else it was early afternoon. Then I directed my attention to Fletcher and Thomas. "You're both here—why?"

I knew it probably came off as rude, but I felt like it was necessary to address the massive elephant in the room—*When had we started trusting Fletcher?* I mean, I suppose we'd never specifically said we didn't, but it was implied since he was working for his father.

Rachel squeezed Fletcher's hand as she settled between her two mates. She seemed like she was literally glowing, and no matter what was going on, the joy that radiated off of her made me happy in return. Something had clearly been repaired between the three of them.

"We originally came here to clarify our part in all of this, especially once we heard you'd met with other council leaders," Fletcher explained, shifting uncomfortably in his seat. "My brother made me realize that the way I'd been conducting things could have come across as me siding with my father— agreeing with what he's been doing."

"And that is anything but the case," Thomas stated.

"What do you mean?" I asked.

"I've been actively working to remove my father from power since I was sixteen. It's a slow-moving process, but it's been my only focus...well, until I met Rachel. Since meeting her, my only concern was keeping her away from him, no matter what."

It was essentially the same thing he'd said at school—except for the very important distinction that he wasn't just putting up with his father, trying to quietly change the pack's culture from behind the scenes, but *actively working to remove his father from power*. Now I had a better idea of why Rachel had forgiven him.

"So once we heard of the other council meeting, we decided it was necessary to come here and show that we're on your side as much as the other territory leaders, if not more," Thomas said.

"And now that we know the truth about what he was after and his part in the extermination of the Flash Clan?" Fletcher's gaze turned dark. "I'm more ready than ever to take him down."

"As we mentioned before, you won't find any disagreement on our end." Breaker chuckled, the sound causing me to shiver.

"But we need to be careful about this," Gage warned. "If your father feels threatened or gets wind of this, any chance of finding Bexley's parents may be obsolete."

"I may have an idea of where they are," Thomas said. "I've never been there myself, but there are only a few locations that even Linan's sons weren't shown."

Sitting up straighter, I kept my gaze on him, willing him to give me my parents' exact location. My dragon moved in my chest, restless, and I tightened my hold on Breaker, worried that I would shift and fly off to find them if I wasn't careful.

"Around ten years ago, my father began the construction of a bunker twelve stories beneath the city. We never saw its progress, and workers would go in and never come back out. The elevator that goes down there is only reachable through several high security checkpoints below the main pack house. That was as far as I ever got before the bastard threatened to kill Fletcher if I tried to go down there again."

"Shit," Jagger muttered.

"It's a start," I said, "but getting to the pack house sounds like it'll be hard considering how many pack members you have."

"It will be," Fletcher agreed, "Unless there's a distraction. I may not know the details of what my father has planned—he's a paranoid fucker and I think he knows he can't trust me—but I know how he works, and I have no doubt he's planning an attack. If he attacks outside of city limits, we can go into the pack house while most of them are away."

"We just need to figure out when," Thomas said, "which may prove more difficult than we'd like."

"Tonight during the meeting we can see if anyone else has information regarding his plans and go from there—I think hearing that you've officially joined us will embolden anyone on the fence," Breaker said. "Especially because you're the future of the pack."

"The minute he's gone, things will change," Fletcher agreed.

"You can say that again," Rachel murmured. It made me smile a little, although I had to wonder if she knew how bad it was. She probably did, even more than me. I knew without a doubt that if the three of them were in charge of the pack, things would be very different.

"Lunch time!" a happy voice sang as one of the household staff approached with several others in tow. I wasn't super hungry anymore, but it did soften the tension from our conversation. The meal went fairly fast, Mrs. Silvershade even stopping by to ask Rachel what she needed so she could arrange for it to be sent to the guest suite for tonight.

When we were finally done eating and I'd given Rachel another hug, the three of them made their way to a guest suite to rest up before tonight's event, leaving me in a cocoon of my mates standing around me. I felt more confident now that I knew without a shadow of a doubt that both of Linan's own sons wanted to take him down. It was possible that Fletcher already held sway with some of the pack members, which would mean that Linan would have even less allies...

"This is big," Jagger said, pulling me into their conversation.

"The three of them? Yeah it is," Breaker agreed.

"What do you mean?" I asked.

"After all of this is done, if the Clanguard pack and the Storm Dragon Clans have a true alliance, that's enough to change the future of all of Trabea."

Chapter 22

Bexley Blackforge

"You're nervous," Breaker noted, his gaze on my expression. I was tucked against him trying to focus on the knitting stitch I was working on rather than the clock ticking down, warning me of the meeting to come.

I didn't disagree that the meeting was necessary —not in the least—but it still made me nervous, and the pomp and circumstance involved only heightened the feeling. Normally I loved getting dressed up, but right now it didn't feel fun at all. Instead, the silver, gold, and bronze dress made of three coordinated panels that fell to mid-shin felt more restrictive than anything.

It was a beautiful dress, but that was the last thing I could focus on.

"Yes." I nibbled my lip. "I am. But that seems unavoidable."

"You've met everyone," Breaker reminded me. "And everyone outside of the territory leaders—all of our families—have already been told the truth."

That this was all really my fault. Still, his words calmed me a bit, and I gave a sharp nod as I put down my knitting stuff. Jagger was talking quietly on the phone, and he walked over and dropped a kiss on top of my head, before I stood to join him. Gage was talking to his father near the doorway, the latter having recently arrived.

"When is everyone going to be here?" I asked, looking between the two of them.

Jagger hung up the phone and ran a hand over my back. "The security team just said vehicles started to arrive, so if it would make you feel better, we can head down there."

"That sounds good," I said, rolling up on my toes to kiss his jaw. I had a moment of déjà vu, feeling like we were reliving the moments before the meeting we'd had at school only a few days ago. Thankfully, this time there would only be people we already knew were on our side.

"Gage, we're going to head down," Breaker called out. Mr. Bronzeheart clasped Gage's shoulder and slipped out from the room, leaving him free to come with us. I stopped only momentarily on my way to the door as Jagger slipped a shawl over my shoulders, and the four of us left the bedroom, the nervous energy between all of us heightening the moment.

Although the energy wasn't truly nervous on their end—it was more like anticipation. They were far more collected than myself, and even through our bond they felt confident if not determined.

I needed to pull on their strength.

The minute that thought crossed my mind, I felt like I was doing exactly that, the sensation causing me to straighten my shoulders as I listened to their murmured conversation about everyone who was joining us. By the time we crossed through the foyer towards the large ballroom that had been converted into a meeting space during the course of the afternoon, I was feeling far better.

I wouldn't deny the relief I felt at seeing Rachel, though, who was talking to Annika, the council leader for the prey shifters. Stopping dead in my tracks, I looked between them, an electric bolt of realization hitting me. *That* was why she had looked so familiar.

Annika was somehow related to Rachel.

"Bex!" Rachel called. I slipped past my mates to join them, Annika offering me a smile in greeting.

"Good to see you again, Bexley," Annika said.

"You too. I didn't realize you knew each other," I said to Rachel.

"My cousin, one of like—"

"Forty." Annika snorted. "Rabbits mate *a lot.*"

"More than probably necessary," Rachel admitted, a blush coloring her cheeks. I didn't know what she was thinking about, but I had a pretty good guess from the way she was looking at her mates...

And the mating marks on her freakin' neck. *When did that happen?!* I would have to ask her later.

"It seems like everyone is here," I said, noting all the familiar faces and trying to steer the conversation towards the meeting, eager for it to begin.

"I think we're just waiting on Mrs. Bronzeheart and Mrs. Silvershade," Annika said. "Even William is here."

I saw that—he was talking with Thomas and Fletcher. Fascinating. Seeing everyone together, from Mr. and Mrs. Firespell to even Angelica, Ciaran Bowman's mate, left me feeling more confident than ever that this was the right move. Of course I recognized that Clanguard needed to be held accountable for what he did and that we needed a plan to save my parents, but to see so many others in support of it...it felt good. It felt really good.

"Where's Bex?" Celine Bronzeheart's voice had me turning immediately, and I wouldn't lie—I pretty much ran right into her arms. The hug she gave me calmed my nerves, and when I pulled back, she looked over my expression.

"Are you okay? I don't care about everything going on, not yet. I need to know how you are."

Her honest and sincere concern had me taking a long moment, wanting to give her the truth. "Not really. I want to know if my parents are actually still...I want to know if they need to be saved. And I'm livid that Clanguard hasn't been held account-able. So no, not okay."

Celine squeezed my arm gently. "We're going to figure this out. And mark my words, Clanguard will pay."

I knew she meant it.

As we turned to join the others at the table, a sudden trickle of unease went down my spine. I wasn't the only one to feel it—the whole room froze with tension, and my mates appeared right by my side.

"Something's wrong."

The entire room rocked, an explosion shaking the walls.

Everyone erupted into action, a million things happening at once. The windows cracked, some glass panels falling while others trembled under the force of another explosion, sirens sounding loudly through the estate. Shouts were called throughout the room as the boots of the security team echoed from the marble foyer outside. Gage tried to tell me something, wrapping an arm around my waist and moving me towards the door, but I felt my knees go weak as another blast hit the estate.

At the worst possible moment, flashes of a memory hit me.

A crash sounded as the windows to my bedroom were blown in, heat slapping me across the face. I barely covered my face in time to shield my eyes. Our entire home seemed to shake under the trembling force of whatever was happening, and the blaring sound of the alarms accompanied my mom bursting into my room, the door nearly cracking on impact as it hit the wall.

"Bexley. Up, now," my mom hissed, her face filled with terror as she raced towards my wardrobe and pulled out a pair of shoes and a coat. I was in one of my favorite nightgowns, the one that reminded me of a party dress, and I quickly did as she asked, trying to

form a picture of what was going on. Rubbing my eyes, I looked towards the window and felt fear trickle down my spine.

Smoke. There was smoke and fire outside. Not the type of fire I liked, either.

Without a word, my mom grabbed my hand and nearly dragged me down the hall towards a staircase I was unfamiliar with. Before we began our descent, I heard shouts from behind us, and smoke poured into the hall like a door had been opened.

When I looked back to see who was following us, the door to the stairs slammed shut, and I was enveloped in complete darkness. As we rushed down the stairs, I wanted to ask her where we were going, but fear clogged my throat, making it impossible.

We'd been going to find Rebecca, and this was exactly like that night...

"Cupcake, open your eyes." Gage's voice was hard, and I flung up, not realizing I was in his arms and nearly smacking him right in the face.

"It's Clanguard," I said, scrambling down from his arms. We were in a tower-like room, and the massive windows that normally created a bright space were blasted in.

"It is," Breaker agreed. I walked to stand next to him by the window, Gage and Jagger joining me. As my gaze moved over the front of the Silvershade estate, I gripped onto my mates for support.

Hundreds of wolf shifters surrounded the estate with heavy artillery, marching under a flag with a sigil that I didn't need to recognize to know who it belonged to. A wolf, painted in black and red, stood proudly in the darkening sky like a crimson blood stain.

"It's just like that night," I murmured.

"This is going to end very differently," Gage rumbled.

"Linan Clanguard just started a war," Breaker agreed.

Jagger's hand pressed gently to my back. "A war that he's going to lose."

My mates were right—and I would do anything to ensure the people I loved came out of this alive.

* * *

Flash (The Storm Dragons' Mate 4) will be the final book in the series and is available for order today!

More details (teasers, release date) will be announced in Sinclair's Ravens when ready.

. . .

Interested in the other DIA students?
  Deva's story - Order here!
  Alexandra's story - Order here!
  Alina's story - Order here!

Series Within DIA Universe

Monarchs of Hell (Completed Series) by R.L. Caulder and M. Sinclair
>Insurrection: mybook.to/Monarchs1
>Imbalance: mybook.to/Monarchs2
>Inheritance: mybook.to/Monarchs3

Dark Imaginarium Academy Series
>Phases of the Moon by M. Sinclair
>The Creatures We Crave by R.L. Caulder
>The Storm Dragons' Mate by M. Sinclair
>Blood Oath by R.L. Caulder

Love Bexley?! Meet Maya!

Description

I have spent my entire life in the basement of my father's church. My sadistic mother and god-fearing father believe I have the devil inside of me because I heal after their abuse. I'd accepted long ago I would die in the very place I'd been born without ever feeling the sun on my skin. Then one day, my mother took me from my father's religious cult in the wake of his death. Nearly a week later, and after countless hours with her boyfriend Jed's creepy remarks, I find myself in Washington State. I had only ever interacted with my parents and now Jed, so you can imagine my surprise when I ran smack dab into possibly the most handsome man in the world. He's not alone though, there are intriguing and handsome men popping up everywhere in my life.

Except I shouldn't be focusing on that. I should be preparing for my mother's cruel hits. Preparing to run the minute I turn 18. Preparing to hide from Jed's leering comments and uncomfortable stares. One interaction with this man and I feel like my entire life has been altered.

Five days until I turn 18. *Five days* until my mother realizes what happens when you keep a bird cooped up for too long, only to open its cage. *Five days* until I am out of here.

My problem? Everything inside of me tells me that those intriguing men are mine... and they seem to think the same.

This is a slow/medium burn fantasy RH that features a naive but strong MFC with a troubled past and a secret about what she really is. Come meet Maya and her protective and possessive dragon shifters! This book will be part of the **Reborn** series.

Warnings: Please be advised that the book contains darker themes such as child abuse, PTSD, swearing, and violence. Additionally, sexual themes are suitable for mature audiences +18. This book will end on a slight cliffhanger.

* * *

Prologue

Marco

We pulled into town and the faint scent of the shoreline assaulted my nose through the open window of the car. It brought a small smile to my face. *Home.* Not the home I'd been born in. Not the family I'd been born into. No, this was my home. A home that my flight and I had chosen for ourselves. Washington State. We lived in a small town that wasn't known for anything except the massive lighthouse it featured. It was why we loved it. After everything we've been through, we craved the peace and serenity it had to offer.

"Want anything from inside?" I asked Atlas. He grunted with a shake of his head before he closed his eyes once more. Our drive from Los Angeles had exhausted both of us and the reason for being there had left us both ready to sleep for the next week. I parked my BMW at the pump before standing up to go inside. My dress pants were wrinkled and my hair laid in a million different directions. What I needed right now? To get home and take a long fucking shower before passing out.

Did I need to emphasize anymore how much I needed sleep right now?

Instinctually, I categorized the one other car, a

black rusted-out Ford, parked in front of the gas station shop. There was a larger woman inside in the passenger seat, but the windows were tinted, so I couldn't get a good look at her. Something about the car made me feel off. I put it from my thoughts as I entered the shop and crossed the broken tiled floor to pay for my tank of gas. Outside, the gloomy sky thundered as it began to spit out heavy rain.

I turned toward the bathroom and made my way down the aisle, only to be run over by a young boy. I grunted as the small frame collided with my chest and swayed on their feet. A hiss of pain came from the figure as I steadied them with a solid grip on their small arms.

"Sorry," the soft voice murmured quietly.

"No problem..." I stopped talking as my eyes widened. My hands tightened on the small frame as *her* hood came down. The person I'd thought a boy was, in fact, a young woman. My dragon hissed in recognition as a pair of soft brown eyes, speckled with gold, stared back at me.

I immediately picked up the scent of sea salt, ashes, and roses on her golden skin. It was obvious she wasn't human, but I couldn't for the life of me recognize her scent. Instead, I categorized every element of her soft, wavy chocolate hair that shimmered with gold streaks and fell to her waist once released from her hood. She had the tiniest button nose and thick dark lashes that fluttered nervously. It was possible that she was the most feminine woman I'd ever met. She was just so damn beautiful. Like a rose or something equally as beautiful.

Then I noticed the way her soft pink mouth twisted in pain. I loosened my tightening grip on her thin shoulders. Why was she so thin? Did she need food? We could get her food. Also, a jacket. This wasn't heavy enough for how cold it was.

Fuck. My dragon was in a protective overdrive. This was bad.

"I need to go," she muttered, her voice raspy.

Was she sick? Why was no one taking care of her? If she wanted, I could take care of her. As in, she could come home with me to our flight house. Now. She would have literally anything she ever wanted. *And* I was going to lose my mind if I didn't learn this woman's name.

"Maya," a voice growled from behind her, "leave this man alone."

The woman shrunk down into herself, like a wilted flower. Her eyes took on a dull shine as a massive man, nearly matching Atlas' 6'5" height, appeared over her shoulder. He looked like a mean son of a bitch, but completely human. Those black eyes took note of my hands on Maya and a yellow-toothed sneer took over his face.

"Get in line buddy, she's a fucking tease," he chuckled, grabbing her hood in a taunting manner before pulling her toward the door.

I yanked her back to me, not caring about the obvious show of supernatural strength, wanting her against my chest. Safe there. My instincts were begging me to hide this woman from him. Maya. What a beautiful name. A worried whimper came from her throat as the man in front of us grew red in the face.

"It's fine," she mumbled softly before stepping out from behind my back.

Why was she resigned to his obvious disrespect? I didn't think this man was her father, but who was he then? Was this the person put in charge of watching her? I slipped a thin business card into her jogger pockets and realized she was even thinner than I'd assumed. God. I wanted to help her, but the look in her eyes told me it wasn't the time. No matter. I had her scent. I would find her.

"Come on little bitch, back to the car," the man snarled before herding her out the door. She looked back only once before offering me a barely-there smile. I felt my heart thump with deep low strums. My dragon roared aggressively in my head. He didn't care what she wanted or what the man wanted. He wanted her back here.

I didn't disagree.

"Who the hell was that?" Atlas' low baritone voice asked from the door. His eyes were filled with gold and the realization she had affected both of us had my mind working overtime.

The black truck squealed out of the gas station. I could see her faint outline from the back as the man in the front opened his mouth in what I assumed were screams. It didn't matter though, I would find her. I would help her.

"That is," I sighed as the distance grew and my heart squeezed uncomfortably, "our mate."

Read the completed series today: https://geni.us/ Reborn 1

M. Sinclair

USA Today Bestselling Author

M. Sinclair is a Chicago native, parent to 3 cats, and can be found writing almost every moment of the day. Despite being new to publishing, M. Sinclair has been writing for nearly 10 years now. Currently in love with the Reverse Harem genre, she plans to publish an array of works that are considered romance, suspense, and horror within the year. M. Sinclair lives by the notion that there is enough room for all types of heroines in this world, and being saved is as important as saving others. If you love fantasy romance, obsessive possessive alpha males, and tough FMCs, then M. Sinclair is for you!

tiktok.com/@m.sinclairauthor

Join my newsletter!

Published Works

M. Sinclair has crafted different universes with unique plotlines, character cameos, and shared universe events. As a reader, this means that you may see your favorite character or characters... appear in multiple books besides their own storyline.

Universe 1

Established in 2019

VENGEANCE

Book 1 - Savages

Book 2 - Lunatics

Book 3 - Monsters

Book 4 - Psychos

Complete Series

Vengeance : The Complete Series

THE RED MASQUES

Book 1 - Raven Blood

Book 2 - Ashes & Bones

Book 3 - Shadow Glass

Book 4 - Fire & Smoke

Book 5 - Dark King

Complete Series

A Raven Masques Novel - Birth of a Raven

TEARS OF THE SIREN

Book 1 - Horror of Your Heart

Book 2 - Broken House

Book 3 - Neon Drops

Book 4 - Snapped Strings

Book 5 - Fractured Souls

DESCENDANT

Book 1 - Descendant of Chaos

Book 2 - Descendant of Blood

Book 3 - Descendant of Sin

Book 4 - Descendant of Glory

Book 5 - Descendant of Pain

Book 6 - Descendant of Victory

REBORN

Book 1 - Reborn In Flames

Book 2 - Soaring In Flames

Book 3 - Realm Of Flames

Book 4 - Dying in Flames

Book 5 - Ruling in Flames

Complete Series

THE WRONGED

Book 1 - Wicked Blaze Correctional

Book 2 - Evading Wicked Blaze

Book 3 - Defeating Wicked Blaze

Complete Series

LOST IN FAE

Book 1 - Finding Fae

Book 2 - Exploring Fae

Book 3 - Freeing Fae

* * *

Universe 2

Established in 2020

AMONG SHADOWS

Book 1 - Court of Betrayal

Book 2 - Court of Deception

* * *

Paranormal & Fantasy Series

THESE SERIES ARE NOT CURRENTLY AFFILIATED WITH A SPECIFIC M. SINCLAIR UNIVERSE.

HUNTER'S MOON RITUAL

Book 1 - Howling Love (TBA)

Book 2 - TBA

Book 3 - TBA

PHASES OF THE MOON

Book 1 - Lunar Witch

Book 2 - Blood Witch

Book 3 - Shadow Witch

Book 4 - TBA

THE STORM DRAGONS' MATE

Book 1 - Blitz

Book 2 - Flicker

Book 3 - Surge

Book 4 - Flash

THE DEAD AND NOT SO DEAD

Book 1 - Queen of the Dead

Book 2 - Team Time with the Dead

Book 3 - Dying for the Dead

Complete Series

SILVER FALLS UNIVERSITY

Book 1 - Lost

Book 2 - Forgotten

Book 3 - Discovered

Book 4 - Pursued

Book 5 - Found

I.S.S.

Book 1 - Soothing Nightmares

Book 2 - Defending Nightmares

Book 3 - Defeating Nightmares

Book 4 - Loving Nightmares

Universe Standalone Novel - Mating Monsters

* * *

Contemporary Universe

Established in 2021

THE SHADOWS OF WILDBERRY LANE

Book 1 - Perfection of Suffering

Book 2 - Execution of Anguish

Book 3 - Carnage of Misery

Complete Series

Complete Collection: The Shadows of Wildberry Lane

THEIR POSSESSION

Book 1 - Sheltered

Book 2 - Searched

* * *

Standalone Novels

Peridot (Jewels Cafe Series)

Time for Sensibility (Women of Time)

WILLOWDALE VILLAGE COLLECTION

A collection of standalone novels about the women of Willowdale Village.

Voiceless

SEASONS OF THE HUNTRESS

Winter Huntress

* * *

Collaborations

MONARCHS OF HELL

(*M. SINCLAIR & R.L. CAULDER*)

BOOK 1 - INSURRECTION

BOOK 2 - IMBALANCE

BOOK 3 - INHERITANCE

COMPLETED SERIES

THE VAMPYRES' SOURCE

(*M. SINCLAIR & R.L. CAULDER*)

BOOK 1 - RUTHLESS BLOOD

BOOK 2 - RUTHLESS WAR

BOOK 3 - RUTHLESS LOVE

REBEL HEARTS HEISTS DUET

(*M. SINCLAIR & MELISSA ADAMS*)

Book 1 - Steal Me

Book 2 - Keep Me

COMPLETED DUET

FORBIDDEN FAIRYTALES

(*THE GRIM SISTERS* - M. SINCLAIR & CY JONES)

Book 1 - Stolen Hood

Book 2 - Knights of Sin

Book 3 - Deadly Games